EMBERS OF FATE

USA TODAY BESTSELLING AUTHOR

SILVANA G. SÁNCHEZ

BOOKS BY SILVANA G. SÁNCHEZ

THE UNNATURAL BRETHREN

Written in Blood

Call of Blood

Cast in Blood

Midnight Kiss

BAD BOY SHIFTERS OF THE UNNATURAL BRETHREN

Branded in Love

Runt of the Pack

Embers of Fate

Wings of Shadow

CURSED KINGDOMS

Ash and Snow

Steel and Stone

VESELY ACADEMY

Academy of Extraordinary Creatures

The Soul Thief

Curse the Moon

The Blood of Kings

*Be the first to know when Silvana's next book is available!
Follow her on Bookbub to get an alert whenever she has a new
release, preorder, or discount!*

To the ones who have known the heat of a dragon's breath,
This one's for you.

Some say the world will end in fire,
Some say in ice.
From what I've tasted of desire
I hold with those who favor fire.
But if it had to perish twice,
I think I know enough of hate
To say that for destruction ice
Is also great
And would suffice.

— ROBERT FROST

A NOTE FROM THE AUTHOR

The events that take place in Embers of Fate occurred a year after *Runt of the Pack*, and concurrently with *Cast in Blood* in the passionate world of the Lockhart vampires and cunning Deveraux witches.

Nik and Samara's turbulent love story is tightly woven into the larger Unnatural Brethren saga. Expect appearances from your favorite characters along with new faces. Prepare for joyful tears and trying tribulations, for the greatest romances are forged by the fiercest challenges.

If these complex characters are new to you, I hope you enjoy watching Nik and Samara's bond ignite. Should their darkly romantic tale leave you craving more, I recommend immersing yourself in the full Unnatural Brethren series afterwards.

Until then, get ready to lose yourself in the dangerous allure of shifters, witches, and vampires. Let their world work its supernatural magic.

In love and gratitude,

Silvana.

EMBERS OF FATE

When fire meets ice, forbidden love will scorch enemy clans.

Banished from a den of dragons. The last hope to save his lineage.

Nik, the youngest Draken warlock, was mysteriously exiled as a child. After a decade away, he's summoned home to Paris where his brother Bram leads the dragon clan. But Nik's world turns upside down when he meets a fierce, mysterious woman—Sam. Her strength will empower him as their two warring lineages, the Draken and rival Ursa clans, clash in the fiercest battle.

The clan's most promising witch. Her enemy's greatest weakness.

Samara, Princess of the Ursa clan, is forced to join her brother King Gavriil Alexeev in Paris. Sneaking out to a nightclub, she meets handsome stranger Nik. But when their prelude to a one-night stand becomes Sam's greatest love, she learns Nik belongs to their rival Draken clan. Will she follow her heart, going against her loyalty to her family?

EMBERS OF FATE

NIKOLAAS DRAKEN

I stand here, alone under a star-strewn sky. The waves'
gentle murmurs wash over me, lulling me into a trance.
The breeze plays across my skin, carrying with it the
ocean's salty tang.

A gust of wind suddenly sweeps across the beach,
warmer than the night air, and it startles me, pulling me
back from my reverie. I turn, instinctively, towards the
source of this unexpected warmth, and that's when I see
it—the mansion on the hill, consumed by raging
flames.

The fire roars and crackles, an inferno that lights up
the night, casting flickering shadows on the sand. My
body goes taut, paralyzed, as I witness the devastating
scene before me.

Even from a distance, I can feel the searing heat
radiating off the blaze. It beckons to me like a haunting

song, both terrifying and alluring. For all its destructive force, there is something undeniably captivating about its raw might, its untamed fury.

The roar of the ocean drowns out my senses and numbs me to reality. The flames dance and devour. I know I can't stay here. But dread and disbelief root me in place, powerless to change the tragedy consuming all I know.

PRESENT DAY

Dublin, Ireland.

1

NIK

Flames rise, writhe, and twist, flaring up unpredictably. The oak logs crackle in the massive stone fireplace, radiating warmth against the chill night. I stoke the hearth, sending up a cascade of sparks. Fire has always soothed my restless soul. It has a will of its own, just like me—we refuse to be tamed or controlled.

But even fire cannot warm the cold indifference I've known.

When my parents slipped away, so too did my freedom, scattering like ashes on an icy wind. In an instant, I went from cherished son to despised burden. My older brother Bram wasted no time seizing control, casting me aside like a broken toy. I became nothing but an obstacle in his path to power; a nuisance to be swiftly disposed of. First chance he got, Bram rid himself of me, passing me off to fleeting schools and distant guardians. And just like that, I was branded the black sheep of the Draken clan, a title I've learned to wear with pride and defiance.

I was a child back then, forced to endure the harsh separation from homeland and family. And now here I am, thirteen years later, sitting at my desk, surrounded by stacks of research notes and scribbled diagrams. My dissertation, a supposed magnum opus on the effects of globalization in business management, feels like utter garbage. Frustration bubbles up inside me, ready to explode into an enraged scream. Why did I even bother with this nonsense?

I rise from the seat, unable to contain my agitation any longer, and begin pacing the dark paneled study.

One glance around my posh flat reminds me of my true heritage—that of a powerful warlock. My eyes linger on the gilded spell books and ornate athames lining the bookshelves, the glass vials of elixirs that glimmer in the firelight. Symbols of the mystical arts I have neglected in favor of more practical pursuits. Pursuits meant to satisfy my brother's ambitions, not my own. I've wasted years steeping myself in business studies at university, learning skills with no real purpose or passion. All to further the family's enterprises and swell its coffers. But deep down, I know Bram will never allow me to truly take control, to be the one in charge. It's just another reminder of how little power and agency I have in this world.

A sharp, ragged breath rips from my chest. It all comes down to this: out of the two of us, Bram's the fucking alpha. He's made that clear early on. And I hate myself as I grab the phone. Hate myself for even considering dialing his number. But I do, because I hate this place even more, with its suffocating rules and expectations. And so, I force myself to make the dreaded call, hoping against hope that he will let me leave this prison.

The shrill ring pierces through the silence, and I know with a sinking feeling that it will go straight to voicemail. Bram never takes my calls, preferring to let his Enforcer handle the dirty work. But tonight, I'm desperate enough to risk my brother's rejection once again.

After what seems like an eternity, the bright beep finally sounds.

"Hey... it's me," I mutter into the phone, holding it against my cheek with my shoulder. "Bram, I want to come home." It takes everything in me to address those words, knowing deep down that Bram will never listen. He will continue to ignore me, crushing me under his heel as he always does.

My patience is wearing thin. I rub my temple, feeling the onset of another headache. The now familiar throbbing begins behind my eyes, promising yet another sleepless night ahead. These constant migraines and blurred vision are driving me insane, symptoms with no cause the doctors can find. Just one more mystery plaguing me…

Gods, I may be turning twenty-one soon, but that won't free me from my brother's overbearing grasp. Damn it all! I'll do as I please, even if it ruffles his feathers.

With a frustrated grunt, I tuck my phone into the pocket of my tight jeans and rake a hand through my hair. A primal growl vibrates in my chest. I release a sharp breath and pace angrily around the room before coming to a halt at the window overlooking the street. Rain has been pouring steadily all day, matching my stormy emotions to perfection.

Heaving a sigh, I softly press my brow against the cool pane of glass. My body aches for the familiarity of Paris and the comfort of Draken Manor. Yet here I am, stuck in this desolate place.

A soft voice drifts into the hallway and startles me out of my brooding thoughts.

"Nik, are you up?" she asks, her tone gentle and full of concern.

I wince and curse inwardly. How could I forget about the girl lying in my bed? I make my way to the bedroom, stopping at the doorway. "Yeah," I reply nonchalantly, leaning against the doorframe. Gods, I can't even remember her name. "I had a good time," I continue, feeling awkward as hell.

She groans and hides under the covers, flipping me off with her delicate hand. I purse my lips and give a sharp nod, knowing full well that I deserve it.

"Listen, uh… I'm going to go to the kitchen," I say quickly, stepping back into the hallway. "Take your time." Guilt gnaws at me, but we both knew this was just a one-night stand. No promises were made except for that momentary pleasure. And right now, the last thing I want is a relationship. I'm perfectly miserable on my own, don't need to add a girlfriend into the mix.

I saunter up to the counter, snatching a bottle of water with ease. Life is simple for me—school, pumping iron, and some occasional fun. Dating? Not in my vocabulary.

Commitment has always terrified me, whether romantic or otherwise. After being abandoned so young by my family, it's safer to remain detached and distant. I don't need anyone tying me down with promises they'll inevitably break. Maybe it's Bram's fault for pushing me away, or perhaps it's my parents' for dying too soon. The truth is, I've always been a loner, and I intend to keep it that way.

I take another gulp from the bottle, admiring its clear purity. Unlike most guys my age, I don't drink or smoke. My sole addiction is the gym—my sanctuary, where I can silence all my worries… and gods, I have so many.

The silence in my house is suffocating, amplifying

the tension of this bleak Friday evening. I have no plans, and it seems even the universe is against me as the woman I wronged storms past without a single glance in my direction. She has every right to be furious, but we both played a part in this mess.

I lean back in my chair, surveying the entrance for any sign of her departure. Has she truly left? My heart thrums with trepidation at the thought of her smoldering fury, and I hastily check the locks on the door. There's nothing as dangerous as a woman scorned—a lesson I've learned all too well.

Somehow, I can't shake off the uneasy feeling that she may still be here. I cautiously move through the kitchen and check the hallway, finding nothing. As I peer out the window, I see her crossing the street. A wave of relief rolls over me, only to be quickly shattered by the incessant buzzing of my phone and blaring Zoom alert on my laptop. My heart races as I see notifications flooding in from every messaging app imaginable, each one more urgent than the last.

Utterly baffled, my brow knits together in confusion and I mutter a curse under my breath. "What in the nine hells is happening?" But before I can even attempt to unravel the chaos surrounding me, my phone rings. And when the name on the screen flashes into view, my eyes widen in sheer shock and disbelief.

BRAM

My stomach churns and my veins run cold. I'm fixated on the electronic display, as if Death himself is mocking me. The flood of incessant ringing and flashing alerts feel like a dire omen.

"What the f...?" I swipe at the screen, my heart pounding with every second that passes. Reluctantly, I lift the phone to my ear and answer the call with shaky hands.

"H-hello?"

2

NIK

"Nikolaas."

The voice comes through the speaker, cold and detached. And then I know. It's really him. Bram. Not his lackeys or attorneys. He actually wants to speak to me after all this time.

"Yeah," I reply guardedly into the phone. I stand up straighter, glancing around my lavish flat. The city lights twinkle through the floor-to-ceiling windows, casting a soft, warm glow across the elegantly furnished living room.

How long has it been since we've had a real conversation? I can't even remember. Years certainly. But this isn't a friendly catch-up call in the dead of night; there's an ulterior motive here.

We tread lightly, our words cautious and calculated as if navigating a minefield. The silence hangs heavy between us, loaded with unspoken tension and unanswered questions accumulated over the years apart.

I hear the dull roar of a crowd in the background—laughter, clinking glasses, snippets of mingled conversations. Some ritzy gala or exclusive soiree, no doubt. Bram always did prefer the company of the elite to family. The sole thought ignites a spark of bitterness in me.

Bram cuts straight to the chase, wasting no time with pleasantries. "Our situation has changed," he announces abruptly. His voice is clipped and business-like, as if negotiating a deal rather than addressing his estranged brother.

I brace myself against the smooth, polished windowsill. Rain patters against the glass outside, beading and running in rivulets down the pane. I stare into the gloomy street below, steeling myself for whatever revelation is about to come.

"Our uncle died," Bram continues, his voice devoid of any emotion. "I'm head of the family now."

Uncle Gert. The bitter man who always resented us, and we felt the same in return. That's just how it is in our twisted family—it's all about power plays and politics, nothing is ever truly personal.

I know better than to offer any condolences, so I take a deep breath before responding. "Congratulations," I force out through gritted teeth, unsure of what else to say or do in this situation. What does Bram want from me? And more importantly, how will I disappoint him again this time?

I wait for him to elaborate on how this impacts me, why he's made this sudden contact from so far away. Only silence meets my unspoken questions.

Finally, impatiently, he adds, "With the old fool gone and no other heirs, the Draken estate and company fall to me now, you understand."

My free hand curls into a tight fist, fueled by the subtle condescension in his words. I purse my lips, reading between the lines. So, that's Bram's aim—to consolidate even more wealth and power in his hands, while I continue gathering dust out of sight. The spark of bitterness flares brighter. I should be indifferent; this changes nothing for me. Yet somehow, it still stings.

"Oh, and... just so you know, I'm not getting married anymore." Bram throws the words dispassionately.

My mind reels in disbelief. *Engaged?* My brother was engaged, and I had no idea? "Bram—" I stammer, but he cuts me off before I can ask any questions.

I hear Bram slipping away from the party crowd, the background noise fading. When he speaks again, his voice is hushed with secrecy.

"Listen, Uncle Gert's departure from this world was... *controversial,* to say the least..." he murmurs wryly. "Taking over his estate will surely bring its own set of challenges, as my legitimacy is questioned by those who seek to undermine my rule."

I can't restrain a flare of vicious satisfaction at the thought of the great and mighty Bram facing contested power for once. But I force the unworthy feeling down. Now is not the time to relish in his struggles, however tempting.

"What do you need?" I ask evenly, keeping my voice carefully neutral.

"You. Here." He gives no further details. Of course —Bram expects me to come running from across an ocean the instant he crooks his finger, no questions asked. Resume my role as the obedient younger brother despite the years of silence stretching between us... Typical Bram.

I bristle at his commanding, arrogant tone. "Here?" I ask tightly. Does he mean Paris, London, New York? For a week to prop up appearances? Months mired as a pawn in Draken family politics? As always, he provides no specifics, keeping me blind and pliable to his will. It's infuriating.

I take a slow breath, tamping down the resentment bubbling up inside me. "Alright," I reply evenly. Choosing uneasy peace over provoking futile conflict. For now.

"I'm putting you on the first flight to Paris tomorrow," Bram declares briskly. "I'll have an assistant courier the details."

And with that, he terminates the call abruptly. No forewarning, no chance to negotiate terms or logistics. Just an imperial command expecting unquestioning obedience. I lower the phone, stare at the blank screen. The spark of anger flares, then surges into an open flame.

Damn him! Why does Bram always treat me like an afterthought? A pawn to be shuffled around his board on a whim? He's my own brother, for gods' sake! But apparently, our blood means nothing to him.

Fury surges through me, molten in my veins. My chest heaves as breathing quickens, heart hammering against my ribs. My jaw sets with such force that I let out a growl from the back of my throat. Some primal instinct takes over, my fingers clenching around the phone in a white-knuckled grip.

There's a loud crack, sharp plastic biting into my palm. I stare down at the crushed device, mangled beyond repair. Slowly, I uncurl my fingers, stunned. I did this? With what hidden strength? I'm definitely not on steroids or any performance enhancers.

I step back, phone shards littering the carpet like glittering confetti. "What the hell?" I mutter, shaken. First the bombshell call, now this unexplained force rising from deep within me.

I don't have time to dwell on it. I know Bram will expect compliance, no matter how I might wish to resist his control. For now, I have no choice but to play the obedient brother once more.

As I examine the ruined device, a notification pops up on the broken screen. "Oh, come on! Seriously?" I squint, trying to make out the words through the shattered glass. *Dammit, now I have to get a new phone.*

My wristwatch lights up with an alert—the promised travel details. I read the flight information and let out a string of curses. I have barely enough time to shove some clothes in a suitcase before the car arrives to convey me to this new prison.

I slam the useless phone on the counter and rush to my bedroom, adrenaline pumping through me. One thought ricochets through my mind as I pack hurriedly —perhaps in Paris I can finally regain some small freedom for myself outside Bram's suffocating web. It's a slim hope, but right now, it's all I have to cling to.

3

NIK

Paris, France.

*H*ome. Is this what it's supposed to feel
like?

I sneer at the massive estate before me, feeling like
an unwelcome intruder in a museum of my past.
Memories of my childhood and parents should come
flooding back, but there's only a blank void. The driver
dumps my suitcase unceremoniously at the entrance as a
suited man stands waiting. My heart races with nerves
and anticipation—I haven't seen my brother in over ten
years. As I step through the threshold, the man with salt
and pepper hair gestures for me to follow, his eyes

betraying a hint of curiosity about this long-lost prodigal son.

I yank off my leather jacket the instant I step through the doors. The house is like an inferno, but I welcome the heat after traveling in the chilly night air. A roaring fire crackles at the end of the spacious hall, drawing me in with its flickering tongues. Fire has always calmed my restless soul, and now, on the brink of seeing Bram, it soothes me even more.

"The esteemed M. Draken will see you tomorrow," a man announces in a formal tone.

"Sean will escort you to your room," another adds, gesturing towards a grand staircase.

I tear my gaze away from the hypnotic flames dancing in the massive stone fireplace. "Tomorrow?" I repeat, my voice echoing off the ornate gilded walls. "I was expecting to see my brother tonight."

"M. Draken is currently out at the countryside estate," the man replies tonelessly. "He will return tomorrow for you to meet with him."

My teeth grind together in frustration. Am I to be treated like a child, another pawn in Bram's game? No way in hell. The moment I get settled here, I'll be finding my own place. And I refuse to be cooped up in this mansion, waiting for Bram to grace us with his presence whenever he feels like it.

"I need a car," I state, straightening to my full

height. "You're his personal assistant, correct?" The man nods. "Have a car out front in twenty minutes."

Before he can respond, I turn on my heel and ascend the grand curving staircase, polished oak banisters smooth under my trailing fingertips. Behind me, I hear the man stammering assurances to my brooding back.

I pivot sharply, fixing my brother's assistant with a stern gaze. "And one more thing," I declare, my tone brooking no argument, "I'll need a mobile phone as well."

The assistant nods hastily, clasping his hands in submission. "Consider it taken care of, sir," he replies obediently.

A wicked smirk slowly spreads across my lips. This is rather pleasant. Might as well enjoy being treated like royalty, even if it means living in my brother's shadow.

I stumble into the plushly appointed bedroom, the world spinning with a now familiar dizzy fury. Curse these headaches that seem timed to strike each night. I clutch at my throbbing temples, envisioning my pain melting away through sheer willpower.

Sean, the ever-attentive butler Bram has assigned me, lingers in the doorway looking concerned. "Everything alright, sir?" His genteel voice sounds muffled through the pounding agony in my skull.

I fumble for the pill bottle, my saving grace. "I'm fine," I mutter before placing a bitter tablet under my tongue. Aspirin is useless against these attacks. Only the strongest pills make a dent in this relentless pain. Still, I despise relying on meds to numb my senses.

"Anything you need, sir?" Sean asks dutifully.

I make an effort to adopt a haughty tone despite the hammering inside my head. "That will be all."

With a graceful bow, Sean takes his leave. The taut line of his mouth betrays disapproval at my curt dismissal.

A long exhale slips through my lips the moment I'm alone, the air thick and stifling as a wool blanket in this accursed house. I rush towards the window, desperate for a breath of fresh air to soothe my restless spirit. As soon as I crack open the pane, a refreshing gust caresses my clammy skin, dulling the haunting pain that constantly gnaws at me.

Where does this unease simmering inside me come from? It's not Bram—he's not the spark that ignited these inner flames. This disquiet plagued me long before his imperious summons dragged me back here.

I press my forehead against the cool glass, gazing out at the moonlit courtyard below—an orderly world of manicured hedges, marble fountains, stately palms. So postcard-perfect, yet so foreign to me now. I yearn for the numbing pills to kick in, to grant even a temporary reprieve from this pounding agony in my skull.

Other than presenting a united front for the clan, why did Bram summon me back here after all these years apart? I know he called me to stand as a show of Draken strength against outside threats. But does he believe a lavish room and the family name can compensate for a decade's absence? I chuckle bitterly at the idea. Nothing can fill the hollow chasm carved inside me so long ago. Though curiosity tinges my distress—what else prompted him to break our silence at last, beyond the obvious political motives? What game is he playing?

I gaze up at the night sky, picking out scattered constellations amidst the Parisian haze, like joining fading dots in an abstract painting. Mother taught me those patterns as a boy. One of the few happy memories not stripped away by time.

I close my eyes, inhaling the heady perfume of roses wafting in from the gardens below, mingling with the smoke of crackling birch logs in the fireplaces winding through the manor. Scents of the past conjure ghosts best left undisturbed.

A bitter realization settles in the pit of my stomach. This place, this house that I once called home... it's not the haven I thought it would be, not the warm embrace of family and belonging that I've been craving for so long.

Instead, it's a mausoleum, a cold and lifeless shell of a building that echoes with the shadows of yesteryear, the memories of a life that can never be reclaimed. The halls that once rang with laughter and love now stand silent and empty, a stark reminder of all that I've lost, all that can never be again.

The clock tower chimes midnight, a mournful toll jolting me from my brooding thoughts. "I need to get out of here," I mutter under my breath, a prisoner desperate for any respite from these ornate walls steeped in memory.

I lean closer to the glass as a sleek black and red sports car prowls up the long driveway like a jungle cat. *A Bugatti Chiron Sport.* "Gods, is that... my ride?" I realize with a spark of disbelief. But as I stare at the spotless beauty, I see more than a luxurious vehicle. I see a chance for escape, if only temporary.

Time for a drive to clear my restless mind.

I have no allies here, no friends I can call on in this place that was once home. But the open road and the city night beckon. I need to get away, lose myself for a few reckless hours, feel the wind scour away this lingering unease. Anywhere is better than sitting idle, waiting for dawn and Bram's return.

4

NIK

*P*ulsing lights and pounding bass engulf the crowded nightclub, the music's beat thundering in my chest like a second heartbeat. It's the same lurid scene everywhere I go, yet somehow I'm drawn to these places. I don't dance, don't drink—merely hover at the fringes, an observer. But something about being immersed in the writhing crowd makes me feel alive.

Perhaps it's witnessing others revel in reckless abandon, or make fools of themselves as inhibitions slip away. Whatever the allure, for a few anonymous hours I can forget my troubles and indulge the illusion of belonging. In the crowd, I don't feel so fucking alone.

I push through the sweaty horde, finally reaching the bar. An opening appears and I quickly claim it, resting an elbow on the slick lacquered counter. *"Une bière sans alcool,"* I call over the music, asking for a non-alcoholic beer. The bartenders here usually have something on hand for guys like me.

"Tourtel?" the bartender shouts back, holding up a green bottle.

I nod in agreement and he sends the chilled beer sliding my way. As I lift it to my lips, a guy next to me throws his weight back suddenly, his meaty elbow digging into my ribs. I jerk from the impact, frothy beer splashing down my shirt.

"Fuck!" I growl, flashing pain radiating through my side. Instant rage burns through me like brushfire. I cut my eyes at the hulking stranger, but he doesn't even acknowledge the collision. The urge to pummel his oblivious face courses hotly through my veins.

Deep breath, Nik. No need to start a fight. You didn't come here for that. Just try to relax.

I turn back to the bar and grab a napkin to dab ineffectually at the wet spot on my shirt. As I lift my beer for another attempt, a woman's voice rises insistently behind me.

"I said no. How many times do I have to repeat it?"

The same guy rumbles back, "C'mon, I bought you that drink. Least you could do is thank me."

I quirk an eyebrow at his entitled tone but keep my focus forward. *None of my business.* I'm content to stand here nursing my drink in peace.

Then another elbow jams painfully into my ribs, harder than the first time. I huff out a strained breath, steadying myself on the bar. Molten rage bubbles up inside me.

That's fucking it.

I set my bottle down with a thunk and spin to face the jerk, grabbing his shoulder to yank him around. "Listen here, motherfu—"

The rest dies in my throat as glass shatters loudly next to me. I glance over to see the woman wielding the broken base of her bottle, eyes blazing at the man.

"I said NO," she roars fiercely. "Now leave me the hell alone!"

She rears back, jagged bottle aimed right at his stunned face. *Shit.* She's not just threatening—she fully intends to maim.

"Whoa!" I dart out and seize her slender wrist before she can follow through. Wide brown eyes turn their fury on me instead as I pry away her makeshift weapon.

An unexpected thrill races through me under her piercing gaze. Heat prickles over my skin that has *nothing* to do with anger.

I'm stunned by the feeling, unable to tear my gaze away from her. Who the hell is she?

"Stay out of this, *Thor!*" the guy blusters, grabbing my shoulder.

Big mistake. As his fingers dig into my flesh, blind rage whites out my vision. I swing around and channel all my frustration into one devastating punch straight to his jaw.

The guy drops like a bag of rocks.

I stand over his inert form, panting, the urge to keep hitting surging hotly through me. But I force down the haze of violence and take a step back. When I finally look up, the mystery woman has vanished.

The crowd continues gyrating and drinking around the man's crumpled body, disregardful. I snag my beer from the bar and walk away, shaking off the last clingy tendrils of adrenaline.

"Some fucking welcome," I mutter under my breath, carving a path through the sea of writhing limbs. My skin still feels flushed and prickly from the near fight. Splashing cool water on my face might help settle me down.

I find a hallway in the back, leading to the restrooms. Mercifully quieter here. I push the door open, and there she is—the fierce dark-eyed beauty from the bar.

We stare at each other in the mirror, the energy between us suddenly crackling and electric. I drag my gaze over her alluring figure as she leans against the sink. The earlier heat flares back to life inside me, simmering with raw desire now rather than rage.

She casually reapplies a coat of ruby lipstick, eyes never leaving my reflection. "You followed me," she says, sounding intrigued rather than upset. It's not a question. Confidence and superiority radiate from her very being. And who can blame her? The woman is a goddess walking among mortals. She expected this outcome all along.

"No." The word growls out of me, my body tense and unrelenting in the doorway. I stare at her, consumed by an overwhelming desire that courses through my veins like a drug. She's a force to be reckoned with, a powerful magnet drawing me closer with every passing second... I've never felt this way before, not like this.

What's wrong with me?

Does she feel it too?

She tosses back her glistening mane of chestnut hair. Her siren eyes find mine again, considering me for a long moment. Something unspoken passes between us —recognition? Curiosity? Impossible to define, but undeniably powerful. No matter how much she tries to display an unbreakable confidence, she's flustered, rattled by my presence. I can sense it. And I bet she feels the intense electricity between us as well.

I watch as the stunning woman pulls down the hem of her tight black miniskirt, confidently striding towards me. "I'm finished here," she declares when she reaches me, her gaze already flickering towards the door. But I can't let her leave just yet. There's something off about this situation and I need to figure it out before she disappears. So I quickly shut the door behind me, keeping her trapped in my presence for just a little while longer.

Lazily, she lifts her chin and her stare glides up to meet mine. There it is again. That bright intensity shimmering in her dark brown eyes… What is it exactly? What does it mean? I feel like I should know, but somehow this mystery eludes me.

I don't want to frighten her. But then, she's anything *but* scared. The goddess is fearless. She's proven it only a moment ago. This is a woman who's not afraid to speak her mind, and yet, she does not protest as I invade her personal space an inch further.

Her lips part, eyes flickering with what might be anticipation. Or trepidation. Slowly, I step nearer until mere inches separate us. Her perfume, rich and spicy, fills my senses. I should say something, but words fail me. Primal instinct has taken over.

In answer to the unspoken question hanging between us, she steps closer, her body barely brushing against mine. With deliberate slowness, her hand slips between my arm and torso, reaching past me to the door. Her fingers find the lock, and with a resounding click, she turns it, sealing us inside.

My heart slams against my ribs, the blood roaring in my ears as the tension between us reaches a fever pitch.

Our gazes meet, her eyes fathomless pools of darkness that draw me in, promising pleasure and passion and everything I've ever wanted.

No more words are needed. We both understand.

She wants me. And gods, do I want her.

5

SAM

I'm not waiting one more minute. He's gorgeous as hell, and I'm not staying in Paris forever. Driven by a bold sense of urgency, I glide my hand over his chest, immediately feeling its firmness beneath my fingertips. My heart jolts and my pulse quickens, but I don't stop there. I let my hand drift lower, tracing the defined ridges of his chiseled abs. My intentions are anything but subtle. And he gets the hint. Hot Guy leans in closer, his fiery eyes roving my face before dropping to my body, lazily appraising me. His desire is primal and intense; it mirrors in his gaze and drives me wild with need.

He ravishes me with his stare and he's not laid a hand on me yet. His hair is like spun gold, his blue eyes like those of a tiger stalking its prey—sharp, focused, and fiercely predatory. Towering above me well over six feet, with broad shoulders and a muscular build, he exudes power and confidence. The man's a god and he knows it.

He takes one more step, pressing me back against the sink. The heat of his body washes over me, sending shivers down my spine and pooling between my legs. *Shit.* I'm not wearing any underwear tonight. The skin-tight skirt leaves no room for it without creating a hideous crease. Oh, dear gods... I feel his gaze boring into me, as if he *knows* my core is aching to be full of him, begging for release.

This is not at all the evening I'd planned. This was just supposed to be a fun night out—but isn't the fun barely beginning?

Sheer determination sharpens his expression, electrifying me. The intensity of his gaze washes over me like a physical touch, shooting a thrill through my core. Roughly, he grabs my waist and spins me around to face the full-length mirror. My eyes devour him hungrily, wishing I could rip off his clothes and explore the gorgeous body that must be hidden beneath his tight shirt and jeans.

His fingers tangle in my dark hair, pulling it aside to expose my neck. His hot breath tickles my skin as he leans in closer. A low moan escapes my lips as his stubble grazes over me. The scent of his cologne surrounds me, intoxicating, as I surrender to the overwhelming desire coursing through my being.

My body squirms as his hips press against mine, the friction sending sparks of desire through my veins. I can feel his hardness straining against the fabric of his jeans, and I know he's ready for me. But will he make it that easy? No, I can already tell he wants to play a little first.

His firm hand glides up the curve of my waist and curls over my breast. I gasp when his other hand skims along my belly and dives under my skirt. *Oh, fuck. He's gonna know. What will he do now?* My cheeks burn, but that's not all that's burning for him. I can't stop myself from looking at his reflection, searching his handsome face for any signs of disapproval. And then, as his fingers continue to glide lower, a wicked smile quirks up one corner of his lips.

"Oh gods…" I beg in a desperate whisper. *Whatever you're planning, do it now. I need it.* I can feel myself reaching my breaking point.

Without lifting his face, his fierce gaze slices through the mirror and meets mine. He's the most gorgeous creature I've ever laid eyes on. And he wants me. "Shhh… I'm taking my sweet time with you," he purrs close to my ear.

Holy hell.

His words send a shiver down my spine as his lips dance along my heated skin, leaving a trail of fire in their wake. His voice is smooth velvet. I could come just by hearing it.

His hands are everywhere, roaming my body like a

masterful artist, memorizing every curve, every hollow of this canvas that is my trembling form. My breath comes out in pants as he pushes up the hem of my skirt, baring my thighs and then my core for his inspection. With one look in the mirror, I can see how wet I am for him, how desperately I need him to fill me up and end this exquisite torment.

Suddenly, his fingers dive between my legs, slipping inside my entrance with no mercy. "Ungh!" The sound escapes my lips before I can help it. But in this throbbing club bathroom, who's going to care? Besides, I'm too lost in the sensation of him inside me to care about anything else in the world. He teases me mercilessly, rubbing his thumb against my swollen bud while simultaneously thrusting two fingers within me.

Gripping the sink for support, I arch my back, silently begging for more. He obliges by picking up the pace, hammering four fingers deep into my aching core. "Oh gods," I moan louder this time as he curls his digits just so.

His left hand leaves my hair and glides down my body, covering my own hand that's now resting on the counter. He guides my trembling fingers to join his, our combined touch becoming an unstoppable force against the growing inferno within me. I can't believe we're doing this here, in the club's bathroom, mere feet away from the thumping bass of the music and drunken revelers. The thrill only heightens my arousal as I grind against our entwined fingers.

His free hand dives into my hair again, fingers twisting in the dark strands as he gently pulls, tugging my head back and exposing the column of my throat to his hungry gaze.

"Look at yourself," he growls in my ear, his voice gravelly with need. "See how badly you want it."

I meet my eyes in the mirror, and what I see there is a stranger. This woman isn't the shy Ursa heiress who blushes at racy passages in romance novels; she's a siren, a goddess on the verge of ecstasy, and her yearning is loud and clear.

White-hot pleasure sears through me as I continue to stare into my eyes; they're hazy with lust, pupils blown wide with desire. It's like I'm watching myself from a distance, witnessing this wild, uninhibited version of me unravel before my very gaze.

Our stares lock as we reach for that pinnacle together, to the edge of the purest bliss. My toes curl in my high heels as I feel my climax building—so close, yet so far away.

He senses it too, damn him. As my fingernails dig into the porcelain, his fingers withdraw from my body, leaving me aching and wanting. *How dare he?* I whirl around to face him, ready to slap him, but he catches my wrists in a tight grip. "So impatient," he purrs, his eyes smoldering with desire.

"Why?" I pant out between heavy breaths. "Why are you doing this to me?"

His mouth twists into a mischievous smirk as he leans forward and whispers in my ear, "Because I can."

A growl lingers in his throat, a familiar sound. In a flash, he seizes my ass and raises me over the cold marble slab. He inches closer, parting my knees with his legs and diving into that space. *Oh gods.* He's acting on pure instinct and I'm dying to discover what he will do next.

His strong, calloused hands cup the sides of my face and pull me towards him. Our mouths collide in a fiery explosion of desire, his tongue slipping past my lips and into my mouth. I can't help but moan in pure bliss as our bodies mold together, lost in the moment's passion.

Yes. That's what I'm talking about. More of this.

I lock a hand around his nape, yanking him towards me roughly. My free hand swiftly unbuckles his belt, eager to explore what lies beneath.

A cocky smirk graces his lips as they meet mine. "Nuh-uh..." he murmurs, arrogant huskiness lingering in his tone. "Not yet." Then he captures my mouth in another scorching kiss, setting every nerve ending ablaze.

His fingers burn into my bare knee before slowly trailing up my inner thigh. A thrill rushes through me. I am breathless, panting, struggling not to faint right now. But then, his touch finds a spot that makes me shudder in his hold. I gasp and moan, my hips buckling against him, driving him deeper.

Fuck. He's amazing. If he can do that with just his fingers, I can only imagine…

My body soars higher with each passing second, his skilled hands taking me to the edge fast. The pleasure shocks and overwhelms me, but my trust in him remains unwavering. At this point, I am at his mercy.

"That's it…" He buries his face in my shoulder and moans, "Come for me now."

My core shakes at his command, pleasure washing over me like a tidal wave. It's intense and blinding, rendering me helpless as I feel myself on the brink of an out-of-body experience. In the distance, I hear my voice crying out in delirium as he shows me the true meaning of ecstasy.

He brings me back down again, his lips blazing a trail of fiery kisses up my neck and finally landing on my mouth. I kiss him back with unbridled passion—elated, exhausted, grateful that this gorgeous man was ever born into the world.

My chest heaves with panting breaths. I can't move, can't say a word, swept by the powerful sensations rushing through me. Regardless, he reads my needs. He takes his rugged hand to his waist and finally starts undoing his belt.

Oh gods. Yes! I want to scream, but bite down on my hand instead. It's going to happen. I want it so badly. So, so badly... And then, someone knocks on the door.

"No, no…" I groan, trying to catch my breath. But my head is still spinning.

He doesn't even glance back at the door. His eyes are trained solely on me, a smug smile playing on his lips as he reads my face. He's filled with pride and feverish lust, his whole being focused on satisfying my every desire.

But then I hear a voice calling out, breaking the spell between us. "Sam?" it says.

I shut my eyes. *Dammit. It's Mila.* How dare she interrupt us at such a crucial moment?

I release a long, stuttered breath, heart pounding hard against my chest. His eyes bore into mine, and without a sound, he speaks to me, conveying that he finds the situation frustrating yet absolutely hilarious. I echo his sentiment. And then I realize, it's impossible. We shouldn't be able to communicate so clearly without words. Not unless…

Another knock on the door.

"Sam, are you all right?" Mila's voice rings out. This time, her pitch goes a notch higher, full of concern and urgency.

He bites down on his lower lip, trapping me between his hands on either side of me against the slab of marble. He's unwilling to let go, and I wouldn't have it any other way.

I wince. "She's not going to leave," I whisper, frustrated at missing out on what could possibly be the best sex of my life. The truth is, if I don't come out now, she'll come back with the entire Elite of the Ursa Clan in tow. And that's not a good thing. *Never* a good thing.

He remains silent, his tongue darting out to wet his lower lip. Slowly, he fastens his belt and takes a step back, putting painful distance between us. Without his strong arms and solid chest holding onto me, I suddenly feel cold and vulnerable.

Reluctantly, I get off the slab of marble and stare at him. He's not much of a talker, but I don't care. *I* want to do the talking. *Will I see you again?* I want to ask. *Do you want my number?* Dammit, I'd say these things if they didn't make me sound so clingy. Oh, but how can anyone not cling to this gorgeous man?

I hastily smooth down my hair and straighten my skirt. A quick glance in the mirror reveals my blushing face, my lips red scarlet from his ravishing kisses.

I catch a glimpse of him as he strides towards the door.

Just before stepping out, he pauses and looks back over his shoulder at me. Our eyes lock, and in his simmering sapphire gaze I read the unspoken promise of our paths crossing again. A shiver dances down my spine at the certainty in that heated stare.

He turns the lock, then opens the door wide and walks out of the restroom. The throbbing bass of the nightclub's music seeps into the room, mercilessly grounding me back to reality. And when he's gone, all I see is Mila's pale face turning even paler, her mouth gaping open and eyes so wide they're about to pop out of their sockets.

"Mila," I snap, jolting her out of her daze.

She startles. "Huh?"

"You wanted something," I add bitterly. It'd better be worth it since I just gave up the best sex of my life.

"Yeah," she says, glancing down the hallway. I can tell by her expression that Hot Guy is no longer there. Her gaze flicks back to mine. "Samara, we have to go. Your brother's looking for you."

I roll my eyes in annoyance. "Ugh," I growl. "Of course he is. We better go now... The gods forbid we keep the almighty *Ursa King* waiting."

6

SAM

When the car pulls up to the driveway, I'm clasping my hands so tightly that my knuckles blaze white. I try not to betray my inner restlessness, but surely fail. Gavriil wants to see me in the study. That can only mean one thing—he wants something from me. This is no warm fraternal reunion. The tender brother I knew growing up died a year ago. I hardly recognize this stern-eyed man who calls himself my sibling, the Ursa King.

At twenty, I'm just one year shy of coming into my full power as a witch. Gavriil knows this, though he'd never admit it aloud. He also knows full well I'll be a formidable spellcaster. My magic has astonished us both more than once. Yet, in the end, titles matter more than gifts. He's King, and I the subordinate younger sister who must bend to his decrees, no matter how much I might wish to resist.

Rattled, I turn to Mila next to me in the backseat, gazing dreamily out the window as she hums a lilting tune. So whimsical, her mind ever-wandering to realms only she can see. We've been inseparable since childhood, brought together by our brothers' close bond.

"Mila," I say sharply, breaking her reverie.

She blinks, focusing on me. "Hmm? What is it?"

I bite my lip, fighting to keep my voice calm. "Give me your jeans," I demand, unable to break the centuries-old tradition of our clan, where everything is an order instead of a request.

Mila's nose scrunches in confusion. "What? Why?"

"Your jeans," I repeat impatiently through gritted teeth. "Now!"

Her scowl deepens as she contemplates her limited options. "But then, what will *I* wear?" she protests.

"I'll give you my skirt!" I say, my voice hoarse with frustration. She's not getting it, is she? "I can't have Gavriil see me like this. You know how he gets."

"Sam..." she whines, not realizing the gravity of the situation.

"Mila!" I exclaim, widening my eyes in urgency. "I would do it for you, you know that."

Understanding dawns on her face, followed by resignation. "Ugh... fine," she sighs, wriggling out of her jeans.

"Dima," I bark at our bodyguard, giving him a stern look as he sits quietly behind the wheel. "Not a word of this to Gavriil!" Immediately, my hand flies to my mouth in a futile attempt to stifle my laughter. It's not like me to be so short with Dima—after all, he's an Elite member of my brother's Royal Guard. But maybe it's the martinis talking. Or maybe, this whole absurd situation is just too damn funny.

His eyes lock on mine through the rearview mirror. Dima simply smiles forgivingly. Mila's older brother has been immune to our foolishness for as long as I can remember.

I turn back to Mila, struggling to keep a straight face. "Oh, and by the way..." I whisper conspiratorially. "I'm not wearing any underwear."

"Oh my gods, Samara!" Mila's face contorts with disapproval as she glares at me. "TMI!" she exclaims, throwing her hands up in front of her.

Dima shuts his eyes and shakes his head. "For the love of Chernobog... Why me?" he grumbles under his breath, clearly annoyed by our antics.

I unzip my skirt and hand it over to Mila, her eyes clenching in disgust as she tosses me the pair of jeans. "Keep them!" she says with a grimace.

A giggle escapes me as I slip on the denim piece. "I will," I tell her playfully.

"Alright," I heave a sigh, flipping my dark hair back. "I'm ready."

I'm not.

LAUGHTER FADES TO UNEASE AS I APPROACH THE manor. My neck prickles, my skin feeling suddenly exposed. But Gavriil will not see me falter. We Ursas bow to no one, least of all each other.

Each step takes me closer to Gavriil's haven—his private study filled with books that serve as his escape. He's traded axe throwing for reading. A safer pastime, all things considered.

My mouth goes dry as I reach the ornately carved doors. "Be calm… Be strong," I quietly intone, but my nerves thrum within me like a poorly tuned violin.

My eyes shut tightly as I mentally prepare myself to face my brother, praying to all the gods that he's in a good mood. Lately, it's always a gamble with him. The last thing I need is for us to fight right now. My head is swimming from the martinis I downed earlier. Dear gods, please don't let him notice.

Keep your distance and you'll be fine.

I nod to myself. That frantic voice speaking in my mind often tells me to behave, but I rarely listen. Some people might call it a *conscience.* I call her *Brenda.* And tonight, she's all I've got.

The sudden memory of the gorgeous guy from the nightclub floods my mind… I can't help but ache for his touch, his skilled fingers tracing patterns on my skin, igniting a fire within me.

No. Focus. My brother awaits behind the door and I must be ready for whatever he expects from me.

I knock, albeit less than thrilled. The door creaks open, revealing none other than Gavriil's loyal friend and Enforcer. "Sasha," I greet him with a curt nod.

Seeing him here only sets me further on edge. His sly smile and raised blonde eyebrow scream that he's learned of my nighttime activities. *Damn it.* But how much does he know? Does he just know I snuck out to a club, or does he know about Hot Guy? My blood runs cold at the mere thought. No, he can't possibly know about him. No one saw him, except for Mila, and I trust her completely.

"Welcome back," Sasha purrs with an obnoxious all-knowing tone, ice-blue eyes boring into me, seeing straight through my soul. I bite back the urge to roll my eyes at his smugness, knowing that in this clan, there are no secrets or privacy. Welcome back, indeed.

Gavriil stands stiffly at the window, his stare fixed outside towards the driveway. Panic courses through me —did he witness my arrival moments ago? No, I remind myself, the dense foliage obscures most of the view. He couldn't possibly see through it. But what about Dima? Did my friend's brother call and expose my secrets? Now anger brews inside me, my mind racing wildly with endless possibilities.

But the pandemonium only breaks on the inside. Outside, I remain cool as an iceberg. I may not possess my brother's ability to physically shift into a bear, but I've learned to adapt and shift in *other* ways. Gavriil has forced that upon me. I pray this ordeal will be over soon.

Our gazes lock through the pane's reflection and a shiver dances down my spine. Since the loss of his mate, shadows cling to Gavriil that no light can pierce. The permanent eclipse of grief darkens his countenance. This meeting will be no easy conversation between siblings.

"Samara..." Gavriil says in a low, chilled voice that makes me shudder.

My heart jolts into a gallop. I will be fine as long as he doesn't touch me. As if I didn't have it bad enough, my brother is a freaking empath. One brush of contact and he'll sense my roiling anxiety. I must keep my distance.

I manage to stammer out, "You wanted to see me," despite my dry mouth.

"You weren't easy to find..." he retorts in a low growl. At last, Gavriil turns from the window, hands clasped rigidly behind his back. His broad shoulders are taut beneath his dark suit jacket.

When his hooded eyes lock on mine, gooseflesh shoots up my arms. The oppressive darkness hovering over him has become his steadfast companion since Luciana's loss.

He frowns, taking a moment to arrange his thoughts with meticulous care. Then his piercing maroon gaze fixes on me once more. "We've been summoned to a séance."

I glower at his pronouncement, but quickly master my features to neutrality. "A séance," I repeat evenly. *Never openly question the Ursa King's decrees, even if he is your brother,* warns the Brenda-voice in my head. Grudgingly, I heed her advice.

"On Samhain eve," Gavriil adds, resuming his restless pacing before the imposing desk. The massive bear pelt draped over the chair is his prized trophy, claimed after defeating Grisha, our fiercest enemy, and his mate's murderer. He treats the ghastly grisly spoils as a makeshift throne, a symbol of hard-won dominion.

My brother stops between the desk and the chair, facing me.

I remain silent. Samhain is my lone night of freedom, my chance to escape these suffocating walls. To maybe cross paths again with that alluring stranger from the club...

Gavriil's eyes narrow, somehow sensing my unease. It's as if he can scent the disappointment radiating off of me. He leans forward onto the desk, shoulders tensing beneath his jacket. "You seem... *displeased* by this news," he notes, a dangerous undercurrent in his deceptively mild tone.

I meet his stare directly, refusing to cower. We've been in Paris for over a year now, our sole intention to woo the most influential coven of witches. Gavriil plans to marry into the family. It's madness. I know he doesn't truly care for Cassandra Deveraux, the heiress. This is all just political maneuvering.

He remains silent, but the twitch in his jaw gives away his true feelings. He despises this hollow charade as much as I do. But now that he's unattached and vulnerable, his advisors' constant demands weigh heavily on him.

He presses on. "Is there something you'd like to say?"

My breathing picks up. *Now is not the time for defiance,* warns the ever-cautious Brenda-voice. *Bow your head and obey. Bow, Samara!*

But submission does not come easily tonight. I'm scared to death, but I push through the dread. "I can't go," I blurt out before I can restrain myself.

Gavriil stills, hands braced on the desk as he spears me with an icy glare. Barely leashed fury smolders in his maroon eyes.

"Samara," he warns, his quiet voice strained with mounting frustration. "This is not a request. The Deverauxs have summoned us to a ritual, and we are going."

Of course he'd leap at their command, never

pausing to consider my wishes. "I have plans," I tell him, determined. Where does this audacity come from? The booze. I blame the booze for giving me the courage to stand up to Gavriil for the first time in my life.

He sets his jaw tight, shutting his eyes and letting out a sharp breath. *"Change them,"* he all but mutters.

His fingers spread on the slab of maple wood and his broad shoulders flex, no longer stooped over the desk but ready to *pounce* over it. My heart races as I wonder if he will shift into his bear form right here in front of me.

I quickly glance around the room, searching for Sasha. But he's gone, leaving me alone with an unpredictable shifter. Fear creeps into my bones as I realize I may be in more trouble than I anticipated.

Even then, I won't back down. "Since when do the Ursa serve at the beck and call of any clan?" I clench my fists, feeling my nails dig into my palms as I take a step forward, emboldened by my own words.

Gavriil's head snaps up, eyes wide with shock as they fix on me. "You've been drinking," he states, clearly stunned.

"No," I force out, trying to sound more convincing than I feel.

His face flares red. "Don't lie to me!" he thunders, fist striking the desk with a resounding crack.

My shoulders jump a little, but I don't step back.

I've had enough of his foul moods. I'm taking a stand. And if that gets the bear out of him, then so be it.

"I can scent the alcohol seeping from your pores," he growls, temper rising as he straightens. "Don't even *think* about trying to deceive me."

I rally my courage. "My personal habits are none of your concern, *brother*," I retort scornfully. "You may be the Ursa King, but you do not own my life. I can do whatever the hell I want!"

Years of simmering vexations now boil over, refusing to be contained. I am no longer a child to be scolded and commanded.

His eyes smolder with outrage, jaw clenched tight. "Watch yourself," he warns, pointing an accusatory finger at me. "You're still underage."

"Don't play the age card on me!" I hiss, an inch closer to the desk. Apparently, I have a death wish. "Next year, I'll come into my full power. And I promise you, Gavriil, you will never see me again!"

Shock cracks through his anger. The muscles in his neck stiffen. Slowly, he leans forward over the desk. "I will never allow that," he says in the lowest, deadliest voice. Ice skitters down my nape at his tone.

"*I* am the Ursa King," Gavriil declares, pronouncing each word like a death sentence. "*I* give the orders around here." He takes a deep breath, mastering his fury. "Not. You."

Unshed tears burn behind my eyes as I push the

words out through a tight throat. "What happened to Luciana was not my fault."

The *Ursa King* flinches. "What did you just say?" he asks, his tone laced with disbelief.

I press on recklessly. "You blame me for her loss." My voice trembles but does not break. "I know you do."

His fierce stare meets mine. "Samara…" he warns me in a whisper. "Don't."

But I won't give in. "You blame me for not finding her with my scriving. You refuse to accept that there are limits to my magic."

Gavriil's lips curl into a sneer. "Yet within weeks of losing her, you found our missing brother in a forsaken cabin in the woods," he murmurs, tone dripping with disdain. "Your magic *certainly* did not fail you then."

I was not ready to hear it, my brother's pain and bitterness. His words pierce me like a knife. My breath hitches, memories flooding back in an instant—Gavriil shattered with grief, pleading for me to locate his mate's body, consumed by his desperate need to honor our clan's traditions... and I couldn't give him that.

I failed him.

"I loved Luciana!" I choke out, hot tears brimming my eyes.

His response comes in a broken whisper, "No more than I do. Believe me."

Gods. The way he talks about her, it's like she's still

here with us. A pang of wistfulness hits me at the thought.

For an endless moment, we stare at one another, the gulf between us never wider. He eyes me as if seeing me truly for the first time.

Gavriil's chest heaves, nostrils flaring with each agitated breath. His arrogant manner crumbles as rage gives way to profound grief. He slumps into the chair, a hand pressed against his creased brow, gaze suddenly distant and hollow. My heart aches at the sight of such raw pain etched on his face.

I've wounded him deeply by raising Luciana's memory, however unintended. All I want is the tender brother I once knew returned to me. But he's trapped reliving that tragic day, trapped in anger and blame instead of allowing himself to heal.

"Dusk. Tomorrow," he finally grits out.

A tear slips down my cheek. "Gavriil..." I whisper, reaching out a hand to him, but knowing it would be useless. He won't let anyone near.

"Go now," he exhales, no longer my brother but my clan's king.

With a heavy heart, I nod silently and turn away to leave the room.

7

SAM

The iron gates clang shut behind our car as it winds up the long gravel drive to Deveraux Manor. I gaze out at the imposing neoclassical facade, each column and pediment symbolizing the centuries of dominance held by this powerful coven. And yet, tonight we come to them as peers, not supplicants.

Beside me, Gavriil sits rigid, knuckles white on the armrests. He insisted on bringing not only Sasha, but also two of his best Elite guards. Though the precaution might insult our hosts' hospitality, nothing will dissuade Gavriil from caution since the attack that stole his Luciana.

When the engine stills, he turns to me with brows drawn. "Stay close tonight." His voice leaves no room for debate. "I'm not leaving you unguarded here."

I nod placation, fighting the urge to glare. Open

defiance will only provoke his ire. He trapped me in this visit; now I am chained to his side. So much for my hopes of exploring the legendary gardens and galleries alone... But who knows, given the proper distraction, I may still find a way to escape.

My role this evening is clear—distant politeness masking utter obedience. The good Ursa sister. I will play my part flawlessly.

Inside, the manor looms quiet and cavernous, the household staff given the night off to celebrate with family, as is tradition on Samhain. Our footsteps echo across marble floors left dark and polished for the occasion, the spaces usually bustling with staff now eerily abandoned.

Gavriil and the Elite walk through the parlor's double doors, but I lag behind, a moth drawn to the manor's flickering lights. Let Gavriil deal with the necessary politics; I wish to wander a bit first and clear my head.

My heels sink into plush carpets lining the wide corridors, display cases, and gilt-framed paintings gleaming in the low light. This stately home oozes old wealth, every surface polished to a smug shine.

I stroll along the portrait gallery, scanning the painted faces of centuries of Deveraux witches. Stern, proud visages follow my passage, silently judging the Ursa intruder in their midst.

At the end hangs Cassandra, the current heiress,

flanked by her ancestors. Cascading raven hair and pale, freckled skin—not the usual red hair look found along generations of Deveraux women.

But while the witches' painted eyes gleam with cunning and drive, Cassandra's stormy gray irises hold only sorrow and resignation. Her beauty is merely a shell masking the frail spirit within.

Powerful magic may course through her veins, but her mind remains shallow and malleable. Yet Gavriil intends to yoke our clan to her line through marriage. The thought curdles my stomach. She is no fit match for an Ursa King.

But next to Cassandra's portrait hangs a legend—Juliette Deveraux, the first Grand Witch of her lineage. Her blazing mane of strawberry red hair cascades down her back, framing high cheekbones and piercing emerald eyes that exude shrewdness even in stillness.

Her rosebud lips hold the slightest curl at the corners, hinting at the silent malice she harbors towards any who dare to defy her. Even captured in motionless oil, her preternatural allure will radiate from the canvas.

"Formidable," I murmur in admiration. What must it have been to wield such unfettered power in an age when women were so utterly dismissed? A true iconoclast.

"The likeness is remarkable indeed," a male voice agrees behind me.

I whirl, my pulse rocketing. A man stands casually

in the archway, keen hazel eyes glinting with unnatural light—*a vampire.* Every muscle in my body tenses. Unlike the Deveraux witches, we Ursas have never trusted blood drinkers. After all, it was a vicious blood demon who took my father's life.

"You're a vampire," I state bluntly. My fingers itch to summon magic, but I restrain the urge. Still, if he meant harm, we are alone here. No one would hear my screams.

But he merely smiles and spreads his hands, adopting a non-threatening stance. "I am. But I assure you, I mean no ill will. Dristan Brek, at your service." He sweeps into an elegant, courtly bow.

I weigh him with a measured look. "Samara Alexeeva," I finally offer in return. The old families all know each other by reputation, if not personally.

"A pleasure making your acquaintance. Are you here for the... *festivities?*" His playful, friendly tone eases some of my wariness. Perhaps legends and old prejudices do not reveal the whole truth about vampires. I should judge him on his merits alone.

"The summoning, yes." Curiosity loosens my tongue. "Tell me, is it true?" I search his face closely. "Has Juliette Deveraux herself returned from the grave?"

The story seems fantastical, but if anyone would know the truth, it would be a vampire allied with the Deverauxs.

Dristan nods, his smile turning wistful. "It is no lie.

I have spoken with her personally. She is still adjusting to this century, but her legendary power remains steadfast." He sounds impressed, even intimidated.

Hope blooms inside me at his words. "To speak with such a renowned witch would be a dream come true," I admit fervently. Skepticism melts away, replaced by growing excitement.

Dristan's smile broadens, eyes glinting with understanding. He proffers his arm. "Then come with me, mademoiselle. Let us make your dream a reality tonight."

I accept his offer readily, caution burned away by my eagerness and fascination. For a chance to speak with the most influential witch of the age, I would trust even the devil himself. Dristan seems a gentleman by comparison—my brother would surely have a fit if he saw me now. Luckily, he's nowhere in sight.

As he escorts me through shadowed halls, a tingle of anticipation runs down my spine. Tonight, anything seems possible under this venerable roof. I cling to Dristan's arm tighter in my growing awe, grateful for his reassuring presence beside me.

Dristan guides me to a candlelit salon. Ensconced on an antique divan sits none other than the living legend herself.

I inhale swiftly, the air knocked from my lungs. Dristan's tales did not exaggerate—Juliette's magic presses down with almost suffocating intensity, a tangible force that leaves me lightheaded.

Her piercing emerald eyes sharpen on me, stripping away all pretenses and probing my innermost spirit. I fight the urge to sink to my knees under her overwhelming presence.

Never have I felt magic like hers—ancient as tributaries carved deep into the bedrock of the earth, yet as vital as lightning splitting the sky. How can her fragile body contain such fathomless power?

"Juliette, may I present Samara Alexeeva, your guest this evening," Dristan announces.

I wet my dry lips, struggling to summon my voice. "Grand Witch, I am honored to meet one of such profound gifts and wisdom." The inadequate words trip over my tongue. I can't help but bow deeply before her, humbled by her presence.

Amusement flickers in Juliette's expression. "Rise, child. We stand as equals, you and I." Her casual praise washes over me like summer rain, soaking into my thirsty soul. "We are sisters in the Craft, after all."

This is no dream—I speak to the most influential witch of our age, purely as women and peers. All too soon, it will end. I cling to every second granted to me.

Gently, she takes my hands in her warm, delicate grasp. Her emerald eyes meet mine with curiosity. "Your magic is astonishingly powerful, my dear. Truly a fearsome gift."

I flush, glancing away self-consciously. But she tilts my chin up, compelling me to meet her earnest gaze.

"You mustn't be ashamed," she says. "One day, our world will be ready to embrace your greatness. I pray the gods grant me years to witness it."

Her words resonate through me, hinting at a glorious destiny I scarcely dare imagine. I manage a silent nod, overcome with emotions I cannot name.

After a moment, Dristan's hand gently squeezes my shoulder. "We should join the others, though I regret stealing you from such a pleasant conversation."

Reluctantly, I nod farewell to the Grand Witch, like one waking from a dream. "I hope we may speak again soon." My voice quivers with longing, hoping our paths will cross once more after tonight.

"And I would hear more of your sharp mind, Samara Alexeeva," she purrs. "Until then." Her smile sets my heart ablaze as Dristan leads me from the salon. But her praise lingers, spurring my spirit to soaring heights. The realm of possibility seems boundless now.

"That was..." I trail off, at a loss for words as we exit the salon. The grand gallery's stillness instantly envelopes us. "Extraordinary," I finally breathe. "She's extraordinary."

Dristan smirks knowingly. "Mm. I felt the same, when we first met. Like reuniting with someone I already knew." He offers his arm, and I take it without hesitation, comforted by his steadying presence. A vampire and an Ursa witch strolling in harmony through the opulent halls of Deveraux Manor—it defies all preternatural laws.

As we turn down the corridor, a petite blonde girl nearly collides with me, only Dristan's quick reflexes preventing a collision.

"Oh! Pardon me!" the girl exclaims, cheeks flushed. "I was just so excited for tonight, I got careless."

Despite her flushed cheeks, a radiant halo enfolds her—exquisite shades of violet, gold, and rose flickering like a living flame. I itch to take her hand, to better read the hues and rhythms of her aura, glimpsing hints of the brilliant witch she will become. But Dristan's subtle look reminds me we've lingered long enough.

Dristan makes introductions. "Lady Clarissa Draken, may I present Lady Samara Alexeeva."

I swallow hard. She's a *Draken*, sworn enemies of my clan for centuries—by the gods, we are surrounded by danger tonight. However, the girl's demeanor is anything but menacing. She couldn't be more than seventeen.

We make small talk about magic and the Grand Witch's return until Dristan offers an arm to each of us as he guides us towards the dining room.

Despite Clarissa's cheerful ease, tension gathers around us as we draw closer. The veil is thinning, and something momentous lurks in the air, just out of sight. As we stand before the room's double doors, my grip on

Dristan's arm tightens, steeling myself for the darkness ahead.

Inhaling deeply, I summon my courage and heave the weighty oak doors ajar. The grand dining hall beyond has been utterly transformed for tonight's ritual. Priceless furniture removed to create an open space, black candles providing the only illumination.

Shadows dance across the polished table, set with twelve chairs. Ornate candelabras line the center, their flames flickering erratically as if stirred by spectral breath.

Despite the hazy darkness, the diverse gathering radiates power. Vampires cloaked in preternatural stillness chat with brash, lively shifters. Watchful witch eyes follow everything, missing no detail. Ageless faces mix with unlined youth, predators keeping polite distance from prey.

Yet brittle camaraderie binds them—the sense of belonging to something meaningful. I ache to join in, to converse and forge connections. But uncertainty roots me in place, a moth paralyzed before that alluring flame of inclusion.

At my side, Dristan surveys the vibrant scene, allowing me time to recover my social bearings. A patient friend and guide when I need one most.

In the shadows, I spot Gavriil's hulking guards flanking him. With surreptitious magic, I dash them a message to remain still, then melt back into the darkness beside Dristan. A moment's worry will do my overprotective brother good.

At the room's center, a lone figure stands by an empty chair—*the thirteenth seat,* biding its time for its owner to appear. Even across the distance, power thrumming around him prickles my skin. No ordinary man, but a blood demon, as the one beside me.

Jet-black hair spills across his proud brow, the ends caressing sharp cheekbones that any model would envy. His skin is alabaster pale, making his fierce green eyes stand out like blazing stars.

He stands with a coiled intensity, power thrumming from his athletic frame. Haughty features carved as if from marble mark him as vampire nobility, along with a subtle arrogance in his posture.

Yet grief shadows his striking face, betraying the turmoil beneath his polished exterior. Love and loss war within him tonight, beneath the ageless beauty and disdainful glamor.

Even across the distance, I feel the force of his ancient magic prickling my skin, raking like spectral claws. Raw yet refined, like a dagger sheathed in silk. Here stands a being who could end my life with a mere thought if he wished.

I whisper urgently to Dristan, "Is that truly Ivan Lockhart?" The elusive vampire lord rarely ventures out of his lair in the United States, yet rumor has it he personally requested this summoning from none other than the Grand Witch herself. Who hasn't heard the stories of the legendary love affair between them centuries ago?

"My youngest fledgling, yes," Dristan confirms, pride and concern warring in his voice. "Tonight's ritual is... personal for our family."

Before I can inquire further, he stiffens, gaze fixed over my shoulder. "Here comes the devil himself now," he murmurs.

I turn to see a dark figure stalking towards us, powerful and elegant. So this is the fabled Ivan. His piercing jade eyes burn with quiet outrage as they set on his maker.

"Dristan?" he asks imperiously. "What is the meaning of this?" His smooth voice drips condescension.

I bristle at his arrogant tone, though we've barely met. Clearly, the rumors of his haughty temperament ring true.

Lockhart's searing gaze bounces from me to young Clarissa. Just then, I notice Gavriil watching us from across the room, his expression hardening. He's ready to break up this meeting in the most hot-headed way. I need to get out of this situation before he causes a scene over nothing.

Dristan remains unruffled, accustomed to his mercurial fledgling's moods. "I met these lovely ladies outside. This is Miss Clarissa Draken and—"

I interrupt with a decisive step forward, my voice laced with urgency. "Shall we proceed? I'd like to get over with this quickly." I put on a snobbish mask as I saunter away and join my brother. His hand finds mine almost immediately, and I know full well there will be consequences for my audacious behavior.

"We'll talk about this later," Gavriil murmurs in my ear, a quiet promise underlying the mild words. My stomach drops—that conversation will be anything but pleasant.

But my chaotic thoughts come to stillness as Juliette's commanding voice echoes off the marble floors and gilded walls, calling all creatures to listen and obey. The very air hums with gathering might in answer.

"Come, let's take our seats." Gavriil leads me through the horde. He pulls back the head chair opposite Juliette's seat and I sit beside him—the Ursa Princess that plays by the king's rules, if only for this evening.

8

NIK

A cool misting rain trickles down as I make my way back to Draken Manor, the quiet night enveloping me, soothing away the restlessness that has plagued my soul for as long as I can remember.

Today has been a journey of rediscovery as I meandered the vibrant streets of Paris on foot for the first time in over a decade. I indulged in a leisurely meal on the bustling Champs-Élysées, watching well-dressed Parisians rush by. Later on, at the Louvre, I marveled at artifacts of my lineage's storied past—ancient texts referencing other dragon shifter clans, including the enigmatic Drachenstein clan, medieval tapestries depicting fierce warriors with our family crests, paintings of my ancestors, including the formidable Lord Willem van Draken. In one wing, our family's more recent history unfolded through displays about my grandfather's business empire and philanthropy.

I lingered in that modern wing, gazing up at photos of my parents cutting ribbons at various grand openings and charity balls, forever immortalized in their youth and idealism before tragedy struck. Bittersweet nostalgia overwhelmed me, there in that quiet gallery housing remnants of the dynasty I was born into but which still feels alien, like glancing at strangers wearing familiar faces.

As I stroll along the serene banks of the Seine, streetlights casting wavering reflections on the inky water, I can't help but reflect on that history. Our clan first came to the City of Lights centuries ago upon the marriage of Dutch dragon shifter Willem Draken to the renowned French enchantress, Juliette Deveraux.

In the greatest time of turmoil for our kind, their union brought together two powerful magical bloodlines and sealed our family's ties to Paris. Though our noble ancestry now feels distant to me, this city has been Draken home ever since. I was but a boy when I last laid eyes on its aesthetic streets and ancient buildings wearing the marks of time with dignity.

Much has changed in the intervening years, for both the Drakens and me. Yet in the evening's soft hush, I feel the strands of the past whispering to me, reminding me that I still belong, if only I dare to reach out and grasp them. This place holds the missing fragments of myself, if I can find the will to seek them out and make myself whole once more.

And yet, the artifacts of my ancestors' towering legacies only sharpen my sense of inadequacy, the enormity of their shadows in which I languish. I am the scion of a revered lineage, yet I have built nothing that could be placed in a museum wing carrying my name.

Alpha or not, the burden of a legacy rests upon the shoulders of its heirs. As I ponder this heavy responsibility, my thoughts turn unbidden to passionate maroon eyes—framed by long, dark lashes fluttering in blissful rapture. Is it possible that one day I will find a woman who ignites my soul as fiercely? A love that could rival the enduring legacies of my ancestors? For now, she remains a tantalizing phantom, teasing my imagination with promises of a future beyond measure.

The more I think about the alluring stranger from last night, the more it haunts me that I may never see her again. Fuck. The thought leaves an ache in my chest. In a sprawling city like Paris, the odds of us crossing paths again feel vanishingly small.

I should have acted before we parted ways, taken some leap into the unknown. But what was I supposed to say—"Thanks for the mind-blowing experience, let's do it again soon?" No, I couldn't be so crass with her. I curse myself as a fool, afraid to grasp what I desired in the moment. And she didn't offer her number either, so I'm not alone in my hesitation…

Sam. That's what her friend called her when she cut short our tryst. An incomplete fragment. But now that name is emblazoned in my mind, seared into my very soul. I turn it over and over, savoring the way it feels on my tongue, the way it echoes in my heart.

Sam. Short and sweet, a name that suits her perfectly. But what could it be short for? Samantha, perhaps? Or maybe something more unique, like Samira or Sammia?

I lift my gaze and take in the daunting silhouette of Draken Manor against the clear moonlit sky. A clash of emotions stirs within me at the sight. The house stands cold and lifeless now, yet hints of the warmth it used to hold still remain.

I've been away long enough that the old traditions feel distant, like childhood toys packed safely in the attic. But I cling to a few cherished memories—the spiced aroma of burning Yule logs, dancing wildly around Beltane bonfires, feeling unfettered joy and belonging.

I climb the manor steps, hands buried in my pockets against the damp chill. Wisps of white mist sail from my lips as I exhale. The night air bites sharply— Samhain is here. The wind howls with unseen spirits. Not the most promising omen.

Inside, I find the foyer crowded with at least a dozen strangers whose voices echo loudly off the marble floors.

Who the hell are these people? Before I can inquire, the studio doors violently burst open.

A tall figure stalks out in a fine navy suit, his shirt collar undone and face flushed. Though he stands over six feet, I still have an inch or two on him. "I will *not* stand for this!" he declares hotly to the tense gathering, his bloodshot eyes ablaze with reckless fury.

Holy fuck, is that…?

"Bram?" I barely utter as recognition hits me full force. I haven't seen him in over ten years.

What will he do at the sight of the younger brother he sent away long ago? Will seeing me rekindle some fragment of lost warmth? I brace myself, half expecting his embrace.

His fierce gaze collides with mine. "Nikolaas," he states flatly as he strides towards me. My heart races with hope—this could be the moment when my brother and I come together and set aflame the bitter days of our past, their cruel ashes finally scattered.

Bram brushes past as if I'm not there. My frail dream crumbles. Surely, he's forgotten I was even coming back. I hang my head in disappointment when he grabs my arm and pulls. "Walk with me," he commands. I have no choice but to follow as he marches on.

"You're here now," he growls, "so you might as well know what's truly happening."

"Where are we going?" I ask with a frown.

We stop at the doorway and Bram pauses to face me. Under the exterior lights, I finally notice the details of his disheveled appearance—red-rimmed eyes with dilated pupils, cracked lips, a flush spreading across his cheeks despite the night's chill. A wayward lock of golden hair falls across his eyes as he sways slightly, one hand braced against the doorframe.

Several emotions flit across his face before he speaks—uncertainty, annoyance, vague recognition. "We're going to *pay a visit* to an old enemy of ours, Niky." He speaks slowly, dredging up the words. His breath leaves no doubt—it reeks of liquor.

Niky. He hasn't used that childhood nickname since we were boys, when things were simpler between us. Hearing it now in his drunken slur feels jarringly out of place.

"An old enemy?" I echo, perplexed.

"The Alexeevs," he growls, his stance suddenly rigid. "The Bear King has defied me for the last fucking time."

The Ursa clan—longtime rivals of our Dragon kindred. Bram seems convinced they have somehow wronged him, but his reasons remain obscured by inebriated fury.

My brother grabs onto my jacket's lapel and pulls me in close, his voice dropping to a menacing whisper. "Our treacherous uncle wronged this family in almost every conceivable way. But fear not, Niky. As the new leader of our clan, I'm going to fix that—*that*, and so much more." He inches closer. "And that wretched Ursa King? He will learn his place once and for all."

He turns to the group of men surrounding us, their necks bearing the unmistakable Draken sigil—an ornate dragon rendered in stark black ink. The mythical beast's wings flare out menacingly, razor claws extended as if to slash some unseen enemy. With a commanding gesture from Bram, they surge forward and I am swept outside along with them, unsure of what dark plans my brother has in store.

"Bram, we can't do this," I say in a hushed tone, my words laced with caution.

My brother scrunches his nose in irritation. "What are you rambling on about now?" he mutters, clearly annoyed.

Making sure no one from the clan is watching, I grasp my brother's shoulder and pull him aside urgently. "Are you drunk?" I demand. "You can't be making decisions like this when your mind is clouded. Can't you see the potential consequences of barging into enemy territory?" My voice is barely above a hiss now.

"Oh... Shut up, Niky!" Bram retorts, jerking away from my grip and straightening his suit jacket. "You weren't at the Deveraux's tonight for the Samhain séance. Not only did Gavriil Alexeev insult me—he publicly *humiliated* me!" He pauses and then adds bitterly, "And to top it off, Clarissa had the audacity to befriend our vampire enemies!"

"Clarissa?" The name comes out in a rush, tinged with desperate hope. "Is she here?" *Can I finally see my baby sister after all these years of being apart?* My heart races at the thought of being reunited with her, torn away from us so cruelly upon our parents' loss. We should have stuck together during those dark days, but Bram thought it better to raise us heirs apart. *More strategic,* he claimed—like hell it was.

"She's on the jet right now, flying to London." My brother's response comes quick and cold. "I'll be damned if I let those bloodsuckers get their hands on her!" The venom in his voice betrays his deep-seated hatred for our eternal foes.

The blood of dragons runs hot through our veins, granting us an inferno of rage and power. Yet as I study my brother's bleary eyes and disheveled appearance, I can't help but wonder whether he's hammered or hungover after last night's festivities. Maybe it's both. Either way, he's not fit to face the Ursa King.

"Let me handle this," I interject, determined to protect my family from any potential downfall. "I'll speak with Gavriil."

Bram's laughter rings in the courtyard, dripping with contempt and vanity. "And what will you say, Nikolaas?" he sneers, pausing for a moment before continuing. "Last time I checked, you were neither a warlock nor a dragon shifter."

The words sting like daggers. Especially since I

stopped studying the craft at Bram's command... I know my brother is not himself right now. So I swallow the pain and respond calmly, "Our family has not seen a dragon shifter in over three hundred years."

But my brother only smirks. "Yet here I am," he taunts, raising an eyebrow. "As the fucking head of this family. Never forget that."

I stare at him in absolute dismay. Bram's been head of the family for two fucking minutes and it's already gone to his head. Oh, but it's more than that—if I'm not careful, my brother might lead our clan to its untimely ruin.

9

SAM

"Welcome back!" Mila's sweet voice echoes down the grand foyer as she sweeps towards me, verdant skirt swishing around her legs. With each step, her auburn curls bounce in perfect rhythm. I open my arms to embrace my dearest friend, instant warmth flooding my heart. Gods, it's good to be home.

The pack hovers in the driveway, tense with anticipation for my brother's arrival. Unlike our united departure earlier, Gavriil insisted I take a separate car home while he traveled alone. Despite my protests, he persisted and assured me it was for my own safety. The weight of Bram Draken's wrath hung heavy in the air after the tense séance, and Gavriil, ever vigilant since the attack on his mate, would take no chances.

Our clan is hungry to hear updates about Gavriil's impending branding ceremony with the Deveraux heiress. And I can sense Mila's curiosity burning just as brightly.

"How did the seance go?" Mila asks with no demure.

I affect an air of mystery, hiding my grin. "More thrilling than I imagined," I tease as I drop my coat on a nearby chair.

"Really?" Mila tugs my arm eagerly as we stroll towards the library. "You must tell me everything! I'm dying to know!"

I catch a trace of cherry woodsmoke as we enter the cozy, book-lined room. Expensive stuff, cherry. But oh, so worth the aroma.

We creep into the reading nook, our steps barely making a sound on the plush carpet. I sink onto the luxurious tufted leather couch, feeling its warm embrace. "So..." I slide off my high heels and tuck my legs underneath me. My gown cascades around me in delicate folds, resembling a midnight flower in full bloom.

"You look every inch the gothic princess tonight," Mila compliments.

I smile ruefully. Gavriil would have me look my best this evening. Any outing with my brother is far from trivial, and tonight's event was no exception. It wasn't an ordinary soiree. Not only was it a crucial opportunity to carve our mark on the lives of the Deveraux witches, but a chance to assert the Ursa's unshakable might to the most influential members of our supernatural world.

And it worked. When Bram Draken tried to claim the seat at the head of the table, Gavriil put him in his place with a single glance. The dragon may huff and rage, but the bear remains the true alpha.

I chuckle at the memory of the dragon's thwarted rage. "No one dominates a room like my brother…" I muse in dark delight.

Oblivious to my remark, Mila leans forward eagerly. "Is it true then?" she asks. "The Grand Witch has returned?"

I nod, the electric atmosphere of the séance room flooding my mind once more. "Oh, yes. Juliette Deveraux is back. More powerful than ever."

A thrill courses through me as I recall the witch's stunning demonstration of magic. But I pause for effect, drawing out the suspense. "Yet even *she* paled next to the spirit we called forth…" My eyes widen in undiluted awe as I look back on what occurred just a few moments ago.

Mila gasps, hands flying to her mouth. "A *real* spirit? Describe everything!"

I grin, thrilled by her rapt attention. "No parlor tricks—this was the real deal. The entity filled the air with menace. But Gavriil controlled it masterfully."

As I describe my brother's impressive feat, Mila

listens with eyes full of wonder. "There's no question about it. He's the greatest warlock of our time," she proclaims loyally when I finish.

"None can match his gifts," I concur with pride. After a pause, I add more quietly, "Although... I did meet an intriguing vampire tonight."

Mila frowns. "Oh, Sam... You know how Gavriil feels about vampires. Tread carefully."

We Ursa kin *do not* associate with vampires. Blood drinkers are our sworn enemies, a feud that has spanned centuries. They are no different than the ruthless Drakens. Our worlds are divided. There is no room for comradeship or even the slightest glimmer of friendship.

"Don't worry, Mila," I assure her as I fidget with my gown's hem. "He's no match for my mysterious Hot Guy." I can't stop myself from blushing as I bring him into the conversation. "No one is."

"Do you mean the guy from the club?" she whispers in confidence.

I nod, a sly smirk playing on my lips. "Gods, yes. Let's talk about Hot Guy..."

No sooner have I spoken than the doors burst open, shattering the library's peaceful atmosphere. In strides my brother, his face twisted in a rage beyond anything I've ever witnessed. Gavriil's expression is fierce and untamed —his bear ready to thrash in full-blown berserker mode.

Hurriedly, he sheds his ebony fur coat and slams it down onto the desk. His fingers grasp at his necktie, yanking it off in a fit of frustration before discarding it carelessly. As he loosens his shirt's collar, I catch a glimpse of the corded muscles in his neck and the pulsing veins beneath... My stomach drops at the wrath scorching his face. I hold my breath, fearing he may shift into a raging beast at any given moment.

Gavriil turns fast and faces whoever is standing beyond the doorway. "How *dare* you set a foot in my house!" he roars.

My gaze snaps to the entrance, but I can't see past the door. Who is capable of igniting such rage in my brother?

"You've gone too far this time, Ursa devil!" a man growls menacingly as he steps into the room.

Ice skitters down my spine at the sight of him—a man I have just met minutes ago at Deveraux Manor. A man foolish enough to track us down here.

"Bram Draken," I breathe, aghast. Here, in the heart of Ursa territory? *Impossible*. This is completely unheard of... and outrageous.

"You dare to steal from me? To rob me of my hard-earned position in the Deveraux lineage?" Bram's tirade fills the room, but my thoughts drift elsewhere. What madness possesses this Draken heir? Why would he recklessly enter my brother's domain and challenge him to a fight he will surely lose? Is he so desperate for death to sweep him off this earth?

Gavriil's chest heaves, fury burning through him like lava in his veins. His jaw clenches with crushing force, the muscles of his neck cording dangerously.

He spears me with a scorching glare that makes me shrink back. "Samara, Mila—leave. Now." Although spoken in the lowest of voices, each word snaps like thunder. In his rage, I glimpse the bear inside straining against its human cage, claws poised to slash and maim.

I rise from the seat and take a bold step forward, palms raised beseechingly. "Brother, don't..." I plead, fear clawing at my heart. The mere thought of him slaying the warlock and reigniting the ancient feud between our families terrifies me to my core.

Sasha appears soundlessly beside me, gently grasping my arm. "Come, my princess," he murmurs. When our eyes meet, I read a calm certainty in him that helps smother my panic. His lips remain sealed, but his gaze speaks volumes. It whispers, *I'm here, Sam. Fear not.*

I slip on my shoes and let Sasha guide me into the hall, but linger at the threshold as Mila scurries away. Gripping Sasha's sleeve, I hiss urgently, "Do not let it end in bloodshed. Please."

He smiles with infuriating tranquility. "Trust me." And with that, he slips inside and pulls the doors shut, sealing me out.

I stare helplessly at the carved wood barrier, muffling but not fully concealing the escalating confrontation within. Never have I felt so powerless in my own home, my fists clenched tight with frustration.

A deafening clamor erupts from the foyer, sending shockwaves of anger and chaos through the clan. Without hesitation, I sprint towards the disturbance, my heart pounding with urgency.

"You!" Dima growls at someone, his voice reverberating through the expansive hall. "Wait outside!"

"I am not leaving him," a man's voice interjects with resolute calm.

"You're not getting past us either!" says another of my kin.

Slowly, I push through the gathered onlookers to find Dima confronting a broad-shouldered stranger, warning him away with a dangerous growl.

"Get out of my way," the man demands, unfazed by the imposing figures of my brothers. It takes guts to stand up to a pack of seven-foot-tall bear shifters.

But I can't let this escalate. There will be no bloodshed in our home.

Before violence can erupt, I step between them, gently pulling Dima's arm down. As I turn to face the defiant intruder, the air leaves my lungs in a rush.

No, it cannot be.

Yet here he stands—the man from the club, his

piercing azure eyes unmistakable. Heat floods my veins at the sight.

Hot Guy.

Hot Guy is in my home.

"You..." I breathe in wonder, the rest of the world fading away. Only he remains in sharp focus.

10

NIK

My every conviction shatters the instant I lay eyes on her—the mysterious siren from the club. What is she doing here, in the lair of the Ursa? I blink hard, certain she must be a vision conjured up by my longing.

But the goddess remains before me in the flesh. Our stares lock, raw shock reflected between us. She worries her full lower lip with even white teeth, hesitation at war with boldness in her gleaming chestnut eyes.

Without a word, she slips through the line of hulking guards blocking my path. They are granite cliffs; she the sea slipping smoothly between them. Halting inches away, she holds my gaze, uncertainty flickering across her exquisite features.

"Come with me," she murmurs, gentle yet firm. Her tone carries a subtle reassuring quality, almost subdued.

When she lowers her eyes demurely, I realize it is my temper she seeks to tame, not my courage. For the sake of peace, I will let her try.

Somehow, she sees through my facade of calm and glimpses the furious blaze kindling wildly inside me. I'm desperate to join my brother as he recklessly confronts the Ursa king—what the hell is Bram thinking? This must be the most foolish thing he's ever done.

But now she's here, and my thoughts turn to her, mystified and enthralled.

"Please," she adds softly, her gaze tentatively meeting mine again. The quiet plea in her chestnut eyes crumbles my resistance. Helpless, I nod mutely and follow as she turns, leading us away from the bristling standoff in the foyer.

My mind churns as I trail her, struggling to align reality with memory. She, here in the bears' den? How can this be?

We pause before a brawny, wild-bearded behemoth whose craggy features are creased with worry. "Samara—" he starts protectively.

"It's alright, Dima," she soothes without hesitation. "I'll be fine." Her calm self-assurance seems to mollify the towering guard. With one last uncertain look at me, he steps aside.

She slips out the front door, trusting I will follow. And so I do, helpless as iron filings to her magnet. Questions race through my mind, but I swallow them back. All that matters is staying close to her, as if she's a dream that could evaporate at any second.

We stand alone on the manor's porch. Unlike me, my clan didn't make it past the gates of this Ursa fortress —what does that say about *them*?

The chilly night air raises gooseflesh on my arms. But greater shivers come from her nearness, a captivating creature I never imagined seeing again. Bathed in silvery moonlight filtering through an ancient oak, she steals the very breath from my lungs.

Her off-the-shoulder satin gown clings flawlessly to every curve, its rich blackness setting off the creamy rose glow of her skin. Lustrous chestnut hair spills around her bare shoulders in tousled waves, begging to be touched. She is resplendent, unreal—too exquisite to be of this earth.

I can't help but admire her straight, delicate nose and full, rosy lips that teased my fantasies for days. The memory of kissing them with fervor in the darkened club floods my mind, followed swiftly by the acute wish to reclaim them now. With great effort, I force my hungry gaze back to her questioning eyes.

I lick my dry lips, pulse racing out of control. "What are you doing here?" I manage to rasp out, my voice rough with barely leashed desire.

She clasps her hands before her, lowering her eyes as if suddenly bashful. "I... I live here," she admits softly. I can tell by her expression that she's as shocked as I am.

Her hushed confession confuses me further. I shake my head in denial. "What? No. That's impossible—this is Gavriil Alexeev's estate."

Her delicate brows rise ever so slightly as our gazes lock. "Yeah…" she exhales, her voice barely above a whisper. "And I am his sister."

Ice skitters down my nape at the sound of those words.

Her pale cheeks bloom crimson as she daringly studies my reaction. I suck in a sharp breath, grappling to accept this bombshell revelation. "Jesus-fucking-Christ…" I mumble—and I'm not even Catholic. The fates toy with me cruelly. She is forbidden fruit on the most dangerous branch of all. But surely our paths crossing again is more than mere chance. It must be destiny intervening, no matter how star-crossed.

"Why are *you* here?" she asks hesitantly. Her tone holds no accusation, only bare curiosity tinged with apprehension. She worries about what my uninvited presence means for her family. If only she knew that I, too, fear this collision of worlds that should never have met.

"I came with Bram," I explain simply, still dazzled by her hypnotic presence. At the mention of my reckless brother, panic flashes in her expressive eyes. She presses a hand to her mouth, slender shoulders tensing.

"Please tell me you are merely his driver," she whispers through her fingers, fear cracking her melodic voice.

The plea wrenches my heart, but I cannot lie. "He is my brother," I confess gently.

She inhales sharply, the truth landing like a physical blow. Silent tears pool in her luminous eyes. "No, no..." she breathes, horrified. "This cannot be happening."

I rake a hand through my hair, turmoil churning within me. "Draken and Alexeev," I muse bitterly. "Of course." Cruel fate would bind me to the one woman whose clan has sworn vengeance against mine for centuries untold. Any union between us could only end in tragedy, like something from the bloodiest tales of old.

Fierce protectiveness wars with despair inside me. She seems so delicate, trembling like a frightened doe before a hunter's bow. But there is an undeniable ferocity in her spirit—I glimpsed it that night we came together so passionately. If only I could shelter her from the bitter storms to come.

But the words stick in my throat. *I am the enemy*— she has no reason to trust me.

"Your name is Samara," I say instead, savoring the sweet taste of it on my tongue. Her full name at last; now irrevocably seared into my mind.

A hesitant smile tugs at her rosebud lips, thawing the fear in her eyes for an instant. "You can call me Sam," she offers in a hushed voice.

Hearing her grant me such warm intimacy unravels the last frayed threads of my composure. In this suspended moment, nothing else exists but her. Not warring clans or family legacies steeped in blood. Just two souls, laid bare under the watching stars.

I return her tentative smile, a foreign giddiness bubbling up inside me. "Yeah, I heard that when you and I..." I trail off, spellbound by the play of moonlight across her elegant cheekbones, turning her skin to alabaster. She steals my very words, reducing me to a mute admirer basking in her presence. Back at the club, we shared passion deeper than anything I've ever known. Here, we forge something much more perilous—understanding.

"Nikolaas!" Bram's furious bellow shatters the stillness.

I flinch, loathing the interruption. Bram storms onto the porch, eyes blazing with heedless fury. His strong hand closes on my arm in a painful viselike grip as he attempts to drag me away. "We're leaving. Now!" His uncompromising tone brokers no debate.

But I stand firm, muscles cording in resistance. "Unhand me," I demand through clenched teeth. "Go if you must, but I'm staying." For once, I will defy him and follow my heart, wherever it may lead. Tomorrow be damned.

Confusion clashes with impatience on Bram's face.

"Have you lost your mind, Nik?" He tries again to pull me along, but I will not budge.

With a snarl of frustration, he turns on his heel, storming off alone into the moonlight-bathed grounds. Relief sweeps through me, though it is only temporary. Soon, I will pay for daring to oppose him. But the price will be small compared to gaining a few stolen moments with the elusive Sam.

She watches Bram depart, slender body sagging as some of the tension leaves her. Those striking doe eyes lift to mine again, seeking answers. "Why did he come here tonight? What madness is this?" Her musical voice rings with confusion.

I rake my fingers through my hair, exhaling harshly. "Honestly? I do not pretend to understand my brother's motives." Or how two intelligent men descended so swiftly into violence. All I know is that I played some role in this unfolding tragedy.

Guilt gnaws at me when I glimpse her fear. She tries valiantly to mask it, throwing back her graceful shoulders and lifting her chin in a show of courage. But I do not miss the slight tremble in her hands, or the shine of barely restrained tears.

Gently, I take her delicate hands in my calloused ones. She does not pull away. "I swear to you, no harm will come at my hand." I pour every ounce of sincerity into the vow. Let our families tear each other apart—I will shed no more innocent blood in this feud.

The rumble of an approaching car engine shatters our fragile cocoon—Bram's SUV. Sam glances over her shoulder, brows creasing.

My throat tightens around all the promises I wish to make but cannot in good faith. *I do not know what the future holds,* I want to say. *But I will see you again, Sam. Even armies could not keep me from your side.*

In the distance, voices call her name impatiently. Our stolen time together is ending. On impulse, I bring her delicate hand to my lips, branding a fervent kiss onto her soft skin. Her lips part in wonder, eyes shining.

"I must go." She turns back, hesitation written across her features. "My brother…" Vulnerability tinges her hushed voice.

"Go," I urge gently before my courage fails me. With a fleeting smile, she turns and rushes back inside, casting one last longing look over her shoulder.

The empty night air wraps around me with a sudden chill. But the fire kindled inside burns hotter than ever. I know what I must do now—follow my heart, no matter where it leads. Bram and the others be damned. I will carve my own path from now on.

Squaring my shoulders, I descend the steps and march towards the gates, towards freedom from the fetters of duty and legacy. The Draken in me thirsts for rebellion and adventure. And I know just the co-conspirator to join me on this perilous quest.

My goddess, my Sam. Destiny brought us together

under this roof tonight; I pray it will see us united again outside these walls. For her, I would brave any storm. A new life awaits beyond the horizon. Side by side, we will seek it out. And the fates themselves will tremble at our combined strength.

This, I vow.

11

NIK

My brother's temper shows no signs of cooling even after we arrive home. He dismisses his guards abruptly and drags me into his private study, fury simmering off him in waves.

The cloying scent of whiskey follows Bram as he paces before the massive oak desk. I bite my tongue, holding back a reprimand. I realize the stress he's undergoing at the moment, taking on the role of head of our family. Booze, however, seems to be the wrong way to deal with our clan's issues. But now is not the time to criticize his drinking, no matter how it clouds his judgement. Out of respect, I remain silent.

I take a seat in one of the leather chairs, but Bram continues prowling like a caged lion. "That beast had the gall to take the head chair from me at the Deveraux's table. Can you believe it?" he suddenly bursts out.

I exhale slowly. "Yes, I heard about the... incident." Though privately, I'm more concerned by Bram's rash reaction than this power move by Gavriil. Does our clan's reputation mean so little to him that he'd risk our safety on a whim?

"As if he were the rightful leader of all covens!" Bram continues ranting, oblivious to me.

I rub my temple wearily. "I understand your frustration, brother. But we cannot challenge the Ursas so brazenly again. It invites only disaster."

At that, Bram whirls on me, eyes blazing. "Do not dare question my decisions," he seethes. "You are in no position to lecture your betters, *brother*." He spits out the word as if it pains him.

I stiffen, hands clenching on my knees. "That was not my intent," I reply tightly. One wrong move could see me banished again. I must step carefully here.

But Bram carries on. "I tolerated your brazen behavior at the bear's den only because you've been away for too long, Niky. But make no mistake, any future displays of disrespect will result in severe repercussions."

I clench my fists, keeping all manner of curses to myself. "Yes, my Alpha," I mutter, my gaze lowered in submission.

Bram stalks closer, looming over me. "You are *nothing*, Nikolaas. No power, no magic." His lip curls in a sneer. "You will never understand what it takes to lead. You are weak."

Each word lands like a blow, but I refuse to show pain. Any signs of emotion could be weaponized against me. I must be ice—cool, smooth, unfeeling.

After a taut silence, Bram turns away, pinching the bridge of his nose. "Oh, but there's more!" he adds, holding up his open hand in the air in a dramatic display that makes my stomach churn. "The Grand Witch *allowed* it. She gave away our seat like it meant nothing!" He leans against the desk and heaves a heavy sigh. "I worry, Niky…" Bram's gaze becomes vacant. "Gavriil is after Cassandra. He means to marry into the Deveraux lineage, and if he does, that fucking head chair will be the least of our problems!"

I remain silent, a cold realization settling in my gut. I'm here merely as my brother's audience, a sounding board for his frustrations. He seeks no counsel from me, no brotherly bond. He doesn't even care that I'm here, standing before him after years of forced separation. The sting of rejection is a familiar pain, but it cuts deeper now, in the face of his blatant indifference.

"That fucking Ursa beast!" Bram turns away, his rage bubbling over. "He's a smug, pretentious mother-fucker!" His words drip with venom, and I can't help but wonder what history lies between them, what wounds have festered into this seething hatred.

Pushing aside my own hurt, I try to be the voice of

reason. "It's been a long day, brother. Maybe you should lie down for a while." The words feel hollow, a feeble attempt at consolation. I've already made peace with the fact that there will be no welcome home celebration after almost a decade of exile, no warm embrace or tearful reunion. I've accepted that Bram will not suddenly transform into the caring, attentive brother I've always yearned for. That hope had been a frail one from the get-go, a childish fantasy I should have long outgrown.

"Yes..." he says under his breath, smoothing a hand on the desk, his fingers tracing the polished wood grain. "Yes, it's been a long day. I'm so tired." He takes off his suit jacket and drops it on the chair next to mine, the fabric crumpling like a discarded second skin.

A moment of silence sails between us, heavy with unspoken resentments and unresolved pain. I feel the distance stretching out, an ocean of hurt and misunderstanding that I don't know how to bridge.

Bram leans against the desk, and his eyes lock with mine, azure irises glinting in the dimming light. "You realize being here is a great opportunity for you," he mumbles, his tone almost condescending. "I could have kept you in Dublin for another two years. But now that I'm in charge, we need to show these fiends a united front." He pauses, the words ringing false even to my ears. "Family is important, Niky."

Is it, really? I want to ask, the question burning on

the tip of my tongue. For years, Bram has pushed me away, exiling me to distant shores and foreign homes. And now, suddenly, he's preaching about the significance of family? The hypocrisy is galling. My jaw clenches tight, so much so that it's hurting, my teeth grinding together as I swallow back the bitter accusations. I remind myself that he's my older brother and the leader of the clan, that I owe him respect and obedience, no matter how undeserved it may feel. And so, I hold my tongue, even when it takes all of my self-restraint not to give him a piece of my mind, to unleash the torrent of hurt and anger that's been building inside me for years.

"Are you all settled?" he asks in a calmer tone, the closest thing to a welcome I've gotten from him so far. The question feels perfunctory, a mere formality rather than genuine concern.

"Yeah..." I mumble, rising from my seat, my legs stiff from the tension coiled within me.

Bram straightens, his movements fluid and self-assured. He walks around the desk and pours himself a glass of scotch, the amber liquid sloshing against the crystal. He stirs the drink in his hold and tilts the glass towards me, silently making the offer.

Don't you think you've had enough? I want to say, eyeing the nearly empty decanter with disapproval. But I can't afford to cross him again, not when our relationship is already so strained. "No, thanks," I say simply, my tone clipped.

"Suit yourself," Bram says, shrugging his shoulders, his indifference all but tangible. He takes a swig, savoring the burn of the alcohol. "Listen, you deserve a bit of fun, I suppose—after all that studying abroad." He takes another sip, his words slurring slightly at the edges. "You've gotten the car, right?"

My mouth goes dry, my heart skipping a beat. "D'you mean the Bugatti?" I ask, quirking up an eyebrow, hardly daring to hope. Is that sleek, powerful beauty really mine now?

"Yeah…" he says, waving a dismissive hand as if it were a worthless trinket rather than a masterpiece of engineering. "You'll have that and everything you might need at your disposal." Another swig, the glass nearly empty now. "Enjoy the city. And when you're fed up with it, you can take the summer house in Brittany and spend some time there."

I am speechless, my mind reeling. "Thanks, Bram." That's all I can manage, the words sticking in my throat. I've only just arrived, and my brother's already planning how to get rid of me again, shuttling me off to some distant property like an unwanted houseguest.

Desperation claws at my insides, a frantic need to prove my worth, to make him see me as more than just a burden. "I… uh… have a master's in business," I add, stepping closer to the desk, my palms sweating. "Maybe, now that I'm here, I can give you a hand with things?" Like stopping him from burning through our inheritance by purchasing incredibly expensive automobiles on a whim.

Bram's brow creases, annoyance flashing across his features. "No need, Niky..." He harrumphs, the sound grating on my nerves. "I have people who take care of that sort of thing for me." He points to the door with his drink, the dismissal clear. "Enjoy your stay home."

I purse my lips and slightly nod, bitterness welling up inside me. "Alright," I mumble, stepping back, the fight draining out of me.

Useless. Absolutely useless. How could I ever think I'd be able to get through to him, to make him see me as an equal, a true brother? Bram's disdain towards me remains untouched by the thread of time, an immovable force that I am powerless against. I don't know why he feels that way about me. But he does. I can't think of anything I might have done to him to make him hate me so much, to treat me with such cold indifference.

"Niky..." he says, and for a moment, I allow myself to hope, to believe that maybe, just maybe, he's about to say something kind, something that will bridge the chasm between us.

I blink, my attention snapping back to the room, to the man who wears my brother's face but feels like a stranger.

"You get to have the best side of the deal, you

know," Bram adds, his voice heavy with exhaustion and something that might be envy. "All the fun with none of the worries."

A spoiled heir. That's what he'd make of me, a useless playboy with no responsibilities, no cares in the world. If only he knew the truth, the loneliness and isolation that have been my constant companions, the gnawing emptiness that no amount of fast cars or fancy houses can fill.

"Yeah…" I mumble, nodding, the fight gone out of me. "Good night, then." The words are a hollow echo, a meaningless pleasantry that tastes like ashes on my tongue.

I turn and walk away, my shoulders hunched, my heart heavy. The door clicks shut behind me with a finality that feels like a death knell, the sound of my last hope shattering.

In the hallway, I lean against the wall, my eyes burning with unshed tears. The weight of Bram's rejection, of the years of loneliness and isolation, crashes down on me like a tidal wave, threatening to sweep me away.

12

NIK

I should have asked for her phone number.

I'm tossing and turning in bed, my mind a restless whirlwind of thoughts and emotions. Sleep eludes me, my body thrumming with a desperate, aching need. I should be consumed with worry, burdened by the knowledge that my brother may have shattered centuries of fragile peace between the Drakens and the Alexeevs. But instead, all I can think about is her. My gorgeous goddess, Samara.

She was a vision in her black evening gown, a precious raven with dark, captivating eyes and plump, glossy lips that begged to be kissed. Her smooth, bare shoulders and flawless fair skin haunt my every thought. I can't stop replaying the memory of her furtive smile, the way she swept me with that striking first glance when I showed up at her home. It all took me back to that unforgettable night at the club, the heat and passion that ignited between us.

"Fires of hell!" I growl, pushing the covers off me in frustration. It's no use. Sleep won't come, not when my mind is consumed with thoughts of her. Sluggishly, I sit up in bed, my body heavy with exhaustion but my mind buzzing with restless energy. How the devil can I reach her? The need to see her again, to hold her in my arms and taste her sweet lips, is a physical ache in my chest. I know I won't find peace until I do.

An idea sparks in my mind, sending my pulse skyrocketing. What if I look her up? *Everyone is Googleable,* a friend once told me. Let's find out if they were right... With trembling fingers, I reach over to the night table and grab my cellphone.

I type her name. Samara Alexeev. And then I wait, my heart pounding in my ears.

A Facebook profile pops up in the search results. Just one. My breath catches in my throat as I click on it, hope and anticipation warring in my chest.

The profile picture is of full, carmine lips, parted to reveal a glittering diamond tongue piercing. Is that... her? I frown, trying to remember if I felt any tongue rings when we kissed. But the memory is hazy, lost in the heat of the moment.

The profile isn't private, but there's little information to be found. No pictures, no activity. Disappointment settles heavy in my gut, but I refuse to let it deter me.

Am I so desperate to see her that I'd DM a complete stranger?

The answer is *yes. Yes, I am.*

With shaking fingers, I type out a message.

NIK: Is that you?

I press send before I can second-guess myself, my heart threatening to burst out of my chest. Minutes pass in absolute agony, each second feeling like an eternity. I stare at the screen, barely daring to breathe.

Nothing happens.

Despair crashes over me like a tidal wave. I'm an idiot. How could I think it would be that easy? With a frustrated grunt, I toss the phone away, disgusted with myself. I suppose I could always go back to her house, but the thought is laughable. Saying I'm not welcome at the Bear King's manor would be a major understatement. Any chance of that ever happening has been blown to smithereens, thanks to Bram.

I collapse back onto the mattress, my eyes fixed on the ceiling as hopelessness settles over me like a suffocating blanket.

Fuck. I shouldn't even be thinking about her. Tensions between our families are high enough as it is. I wince, sweeping a hand across my face as the reality of the situation sinks in. I'm so screwed. But the thing is, I don't really give a damn about any of it. She's all I want, all I can think about.

Suddenly, the phone buzzes. A notification. A message. My heart leaps into my throat. Could it be her? Is it really her? In a frenzy of flailing limbs, I scramble across the bed, reaching for the phone. But in my haste, my legs tangle in the sheets and comforter. I stumble and crash to the floor. "Gah! Fuck!" I curse, pain shooting through my body.

Another message rings out, taunting me.

"Fuck! Fuck!" I growl, kicking and thrashing to free myself from the twisted sheets. In my struggle, I knock the lamp off the night table, sending it crashing down onto my head. "OW!" I yelp, clutching the back of my skull. Fucking bronze stand. Pain throbs through my neck, but I don't feel any blood. Small mercies.

One more message pushes through, and I want to scream in frustration.

This cannot be happening to me.

At last, I manage to untangle myself from the sheets and comforter, the lamp cord no longer a snare around my legs. I crawl across the carpeted floor, my eyes scanning frantically for my phone. If it is her, she's going to think I'm the kind of guy who finds pleasure in stringing her along, only to bail and make himself seem more interesting. "Gods, no!" I groan, hauling myself to my feet and flicking on the lights.

I rake my fingers through my hair, heaving a heavy

sigh as I survey the destruction I've wrought. My gaze sweeps the floor, searching for my elusive phone.

Another message rings out, and I could weep with relief. I follow the sound, dropping to my knees and fishing the phone out from under the bed. How the devil did it get there?

My stomach clenches as I read the green banner on the screen.

ONGOING CALL TO SAMARA ALEXEEV

With my heart pounding in a wild, erratic rhythm, I bring the phone to my ear, my voice shaking as I answer. "Hello?"

"Nik, are you alright?" Her voice is like honey, sweet and smooth, with an undercurrent of concern.

"Who is this?" I ask, even though I know, even though every fiber of my being is screaming that it's her.

"It's Sam. You texted me, then called me?" Her tone is skeptical, questioning. "Are you okay? I heard some struggle over there..."

"Sam, hey..." I straighten, swallowing hard past the lump in my throat. "Yeah, everything's fine." It's not, but I can't let her know that. "So, um... Yeah. I texted you." I start pacing the room, my nerves crackling with energy.

"*And* you called," she adds, a hint of amusement in her voice.

"Yeah. Well, no..." I stammer, my face flushing with

embarrassment. Gods, can I salvage any shred of dignity after this disaster? "The phone... I... kind of... dropped it, and it must have dialed your number?" It's a flimsy excuse, but I cling to it like a lifeline.

"Oh." Her response is short, noncommittal, but I'll take it. Anything is better than the alternative.

"So, uh… let's talk about that tongue ring..." I tease, desperate to steer the conversation away from my clumsiness.

Sam's laugh is a soft, musical purr that sends pleasant shivers down my spine. "Is *that* why you called?" she asks, her voice playful and light. I can picture the smile on her face, and it's the most beautiful thing in the world.

"That alone." I chuckle, unable to keep the grin from my face. "Yeah..." I sink down onto the bed, leaning back against the headboard as a sense of contentment washes over me.

"I'm sorry about what happened," she blurts out, the amusement fading from her velvety voice, replaced by genuine remorse.

"Don't..." I utter, harsher than I intended. "It's not your fault. Bram should never have stormed into your home like that." I pause, considering my next words carefully. "I'm just glad he made it out alive."

"Yeah..." she breathes, relief evident in her tone. "Me too."

I flinch, surprise and confusion warring within me. "Really?" I mumble. "I thought your lot hated my clan."

"And we do," Sam admits. "But... um... I *like* you."

My eyes fly open, my heart soaring at her words. She likes me. A warm, pleasant wave washes over me, and for a moment, I'm certain my heart is melting.

Silence stretches between us, but it's not uncomfortable. It's the kind of silence that feels like a shared secret, a moment of understanding.

"Sam," I say at last, my voice grave and resolved, cutting through the stillness. "I want to see you."

The words hang in the air, a declaration, a plea, a promise. I hold my breath, waiting for her response, my entire being aching for her.

In that moment, nothing else matters. Not the centuries of animosity between our families, not the impossible obstacles that stand in our way. All that matters is her, and the desperate, all-consuming need to be near her.

I close my eyes, sending a silent prayer to the gods, to fate, to anyone who might be listening.

Please, let her say yes. Please, let this be the start of something beautiful, something real.

I've never wanted anything more in my life.

13

SAM

The lights are dim, the gallery purposely cold —a necessary requirement for an exhibition showcasing ancient clothing. I nibble on my lower lip, a nervous habit I can't seem to shake. If I keep this up, it's going to burst open. I try to focus on the antique costumes spread before me, a mesmerizing array of velvet and the finest vintage silks, delicate embroidery clinging to the fabric by the frailest of threads. All this beauty surrounds me, and I know I should be captivated by it, but my mind whirls with rattled anticipation, making it impossible to concentrate.

I check my wristwatch for the umpteenth time. It's not late. In fact, I arrived early, having snuck out of home all by myself. No guards, no entourage. Given the recent craziness in my household, I doubt anyone will even notice my absence. Everyone's attention is fixated on the Deverauxs, my brother absolutely triumphant about securing that coveted head chair at the witches' séance.

"The Opera?" a voice purrs in my ear, sending delicious shivers down my spine.

I turn my head, my gaze meeting ocean eyes that never fail to take my breath away. Nik's lips stretch into a faint smile that slowly broadens, and I can't stop myself from smiling back, my heart fluttering in my chest. "Do you mean a crowded place where no one will notice us?" I tease, lifting my brow slightly. "Yeah."

Nik's warm fingers interlace with mine, sending tingles through my limbs and setting my cheeks ablaze. His touch summons vivid memories of that night at the club... Gods, the magic those fingers created, the way they set my body on fire.

As he draws near, I catch a whiff of his intoxicating cologne, his face temptingly close to mine. "You're admiring the costumes?" Nik asks coolly, his gaze gliding to the exhibit. I'm immediately grateful for the momentary respite he's giving to my racing heart.

His hold on my hand tightens, a silent reassurance that sets my nerves on fire.

"I was," I manage to say, trying to sound casual even as I'm shaking inside, my body extremely aware of his proximity.

We saunter to the central piece in the room, our steps in perfect sync.

"Wow... this is amazing." Nik leans closer to the glass pane, his eyes alight with genuine interest as he admires a Venetian mask lined in black silk, a crown of glossy black feathers adorning its top.

I read the small card beside the display. "Venetian Mask, 1661."

Intrigued, Nik crouches a little, his voice low and alluring as he continues, "This mask belonged to the grand soprano, Letizia Leone. Legend has it the mask was a gift from the Devil, who purportedly granted the singer's prodigious voice." He smirks, throwing me a side glance that sends my pulse racing. "A deal with the Devil, hmm?"

When I turn to face him, we're standing a mere breath apart, the air between us crackling with electric tension. My heart pounds in my chest, threatening to burst free.

"A legend," I tell him, watching him with undisguised delight, my gaze lingering on his handsome face before following the strong line of his jaw. I long to feel the roughness of his short stubble grazing my skin, to lose myself in his touch.

"Yes. Like *magic*, and stories of shifters and witches..." he says knowingly, his eyes glinting with mischief. "Completely fictional."

The corner of my lips curls, pleased by his answer. His family might be the enemy, but it's wonderful to share the truth of our world with him—the world of the supernatural. I sweep our surroundings with a furtive glance, making sure no one is close enough to overhear. "If only they knew..." I whisper conspiratorially.

Magic flickers in Nik's eyes, and in a flash, his mouth seals over mine in a slow, deep kiss that sets my very soul on fire. Liquid heat courses through my veins as I answer with the same simmering passion, my body molding to his. His firm hand cups my cheek, gently pulling me closer, and I feel my knees buckle under the onslaught of sensation. Gods, why did I choose a public place to meet him? I want him right now, consequences be damned.

As he lazily parts from me, I'm left gawking at him like a lovestruck fool, my brain scrambled by his kiss. He's the sexiest man alive, and I'm putty in his hands. Nothing but pure resolve holds me together in this moment.

"Sam," he breathes, his voice low and determined, sending a shiver down my spine.

"Nik..." I beg in a whisper, my body aching for his touch. But then, behind him, a flicker of movement draws my attention. My gaze glides down the slump of his shoulder, and as I tilt my head, my eyes widen in shock. "Shit!" I hiss, panic gripping my heart.

A frown creases Nik's brow, concern etched on his face. "What is it?" he asks, glancing back over his shoulder.

"It's Mila," I say, my voice tight with restless anxiety.

My best friend saunters across the gallery, oblivious to the turmoil her presence is causing. "She's here... Why is she here?" I shake my head, struggling to understand, my mind racing with the potential consequences of being caught.

"Who's Mila?" Nik asks, his nose wrinkling in confusion—a rugged, enticing gesture that sends a flutter through my stomach, even in the midst of my panic.

"The girl who..." I bite my lower lip, hesitating as I search for the right words. "The one who knocked on the door when we..."

Understanding dawns on Nik's face, his fierce stare narrowing. "Ah, so *that's* Mila." He doesn't sound too pleased, and I can't blame him. He sweeps the crowd with a cautious glance, searching for that familiar face. "Is she spying on you?" The words sail through his lips, laced with suspicion.

"I don't know," I say urgently, my heart pounding in my chest. "Nik, she can't see me with you. She knows who you are... If my brother finds out..." Mila strolls closer, moving through the exhibit in a dark purple dress, her fawn hair bouncing with each step. It's a miracle she hasn't spotted me yet, but I know our luck can't hold much longer.

Nik dives his fingers through his dirty blonde hair, frustration clear in his movements. "Fuck..." He heaves a heavy sigh, then squares his shoulders, locking eyes with me. "Alright..." he says, his voice filled with renewed conviction. "Let's go away for the weekend."

"What?" A nervous laugh escapes my lips, and I feel the heat rising in my cheeks. Is he being serious?

He looks around once more, ensuring no Ursa men are lurking nearby. When he's satisfied we're not being watched, he faces me again, his eyes intense. "I have a small house in Brittany. We'd have the entire place to ourselves..." Nik pauses, and my heart threatens to burst from my chest, hope and longing warring within me. "Do you think you can find a way to...?"

"I'll find a way," I interrupt breathlessly, not even caring how desperate I sound. I'll move heaven and earth to be with him, to steal this precious time together.

His charming smile broadens, relief and delight radiating from his countenance. As Nik steps back, ready to leave my side, the brief distance between us feels like a physical ache, a void that needs to be filled.

"Nik," I mumble, my voice barely above a whisper.

"Yeah?" He inches closer, and I seize the moment, stealing a searing kiss from his lips. Our tongues lap together in a sensual prelude to the paradise that awaits us.

When we part this time, Nik is absolutely radiant, magic rippling through his being in waves that I'm not sure he's even aware of. But I'm a witch, and to me, it's as clear as day—a breathtaking sight that steals the air from my lungs. His radiance is the most gorgeous thing I've ever seen. Golden. Like the sun.

And in that moment, I know with absolute certainty that I'll risk everything to be with him, to bask in the warmth of his light. Consequences be damned. I'm falling hard for Nikolaas Draken, and there's no turning back now.

14

SAM

I watch from a distance as a security guard approaches Mila, his tall frame towering over her petite form. My heart clenches with concern, and I take a step forward, ready to intervene if needed. The guard's quizzical glare is intimidating, even from afar, and I can only imagine how Mila must feel under the weight of his scrutiny.

"I saw you skip the line, mademoiselle. Do you have a ticket?" the guard asks in English, his tone firm and unyielding. He must assume Mila is a tourist, and I suppose in a way, we all are—outsiders in this city of light and wonder.

I watch as the color drains from Mila's face, her pale complexion turning ghostly white. She wrings her wrist anxiously, her pink lips mouthing soundless words as she struggles to find a response. "I..." she manages, blinking rapidly, and my heart goes out to her.

Finally, I reach Mila, slipping between her and the security guard. "It's alright. We're leaving," I say, resolved as I sweep a hand around my friend's arm and all but drag her away from the towering figure.

The guard remains undisturbed, his piercing gaze tracking our every move as we ascend the stairs and leave the exhibit room behind. My heart pounds in my chest, a mixture of adrenaline and fear coursing through my veins.

We cover the Opera's grand hall with speedy strides, my hand pushing against the heavy doors until we finally make it out of the beautiful architectural beast. The fresh air hits my face, and I take a deep breath, trying to calm my frayed nerves.

As soon as we're in the clear, I stop and turn to face Mila, my eyes narrowing. "Mila," I all but hiss, my voice rising with each word, "what are you doing here? Are you following me?" If the pitch of my voice goes any higher, I'll be squealing.

Mila's expression darkens with distress, her brow furrowing. "Sam, I had to come," she says, her tone grave and heavy. She swallows hard, tugging a stray lock of fawn hair behind her ear. "I saw you sneak out of the manor. You were with the Draken boy..." She purses her lips, and I can see the concern etched on her face. "You need to put a stop to this. It's dangerous."

"I know that!" I snap, exasperation bubbling up inside me. Gods, that was so mean. I hold my breath for a moment, trying to cool off my temper. "But Mila... I can't." A pause, my determination strengthening with each passing second. "I won't."

"Listen..." Mila's demeanor softens as she takes my hand in hers. "Let's talk in that cafe over there." She points to a small bistro across the street, her eyes pleading. "You can make your choice when you hear what I have to say." My friend gives me a bitter smile, and a sense of unease settles in the pit of my stomach.

"Alright," I mumble, nodding my head in agreement.

When we make it to the small shop, dark clouds gather above us, the air turning cool and moist. A gust of wind picks up my hair, soft strands caressing my cheeks... Gooseflesh shoots up my arms. A bad omen.

I pull out a chair and sit down warily, my mind racing with the possibilities of what Mila might know. And I'm not sure I want to learn what that is.

A server arrives, and Mila has the gall to order ice cream, her face brightening with childlike glee.

"Do you want some?" she asks, her voice dripping with adorable naivete. You'd think we were here simply to hang out, without a care in the world.

I pass on the offer with a dismissive wave of my hand, my appetite long gone.

"Are you sure?" Mila quirks up an eyebrow, her eyes

twinkling. "I hear their chocolate ice cream is to die for," she says, her voice giddy and carefree.

I heave a sigh, my patience wearing thin. "I'm all ears, Mila." The words come out of my mouth reluctantly, a sense of dread creeping up my spine. "What is this news that cannot wait?"

Mila's face straightens, all traces of humor vanishing in an instant. She waits for the server to leave, then leans in closer, her voice low and conspiratorial. "There's been talk in the clan ever since Bram Draken stormed into the manor."

"There's *always* talk in the clan," I dismiss with a scowl, my frustration mounting. "Our brothers are gossipers *par excellence!*" I choke out a dry laugh, hoping to alleviate the tension, but Mila's expression remains flat as a board.

"Sam..." she begins, her stare darkening with each word. "Nikolaas Draken is a *killer*."

Sheer black dread washes over me, my blood running cold. I frown in disbelief, my mind reeling. "What are you talking about?" I manage to say the words, my voice barely above a whisper.

"He was exiled from the Draken clan for nearly a decade..." Mila adds, her tone grave.

"Exiled?" I scrunch my nose, shaking my head. "I'm sure that's not right." She's got it all wrong. "That's not what I know, what I've heard."

Mila shrugs her shoulders, her face impassive.

"That's what the clan says," she rebuffs, as if the Ursa clan were an all-knowing deity. "If indeed he was banished by his own kin, then..."

I'm not liking where this conversation is headed, my heart pounding in my ears. "That was ten years ago!" I stammer, my voice rising with each word. "Nik was a child when he was sent away. Have you met Bram? The guy's a fucking bastard! I'm sure when their parents died, he couldn't wait to be rid of Nik." My voice comes out impassioned, alight with fury and disbelief.

"My brother says Nik killed them," Mila says, her tone wry and cutting, making me despise her, albeit briefly.

I wince, my stomach churning. "Killed, who?"

"His parents."

My mouth slackens, my eyes widening in shock. "Mila!" I gasp, my heart sinking. She will stop at nothing to make me break away from Nik. "That's completely ludicrous! You can't believe these stories. They're nothing but lies... They're the clan's propaganda to feed our hatred for the Drakens." I pause, taking a deep breath to calm my racing heart. "That's all this is."

Mila's ice cream arrives, and it's the most beautiful dish I've ever seen. The rich, velvety chocolate is piled high in an elegant glass bowl, the surface smooth and glossy like a polished mirror, with two golden wafers and gold dust sprinkled on top. Gods, it looks delicious. I shut my eyes and shake my head, refocusing on the conversation at hand. "Anyway... who told Dima that ridiculous story?"

Even as the most gorgeous ice cream sits in front of her, Mila stares at me dead in the eye, her gaze unwavering. "It was your brother, Gavriil."

"Of course he did," I mutter, realization dawning on me. "Sickening politics... My brother's favorite game. Trust me, this is all a sick ploy. I know Gavriil only too well."

Mila dips her spoon in the cup, her eyes flickering to the dessert for the first time. "Maybe you're right," she breathes, her voice softening. "Maybe it's just a string of lies." She bites her lower lip, hesitation evident on her face. "But still, if Gavriil finds out that you're seeing Nik..."

"He won't," I say, my resolve unwavering. "I can trust you, Mila... can't I?" This last part comes out with overwhelming wariness, my heart clenching in my chest.

Mila pushes away the ice cream with the back of her hand, her eyes meeting mine. "Sam, your magic saved my mother's life. I'm forever in your debt..." she says, a shadow of gloom fleeting across her countenance.

"I'm asking..." I manage, my voice trembling. "As a friend." My hand reaches for hers, our fingers intertwining. "Gods, I wouldn't dream of using your mom's health as leverage. Who do you think I am? Ugh..." I wrinkle my nose in disgust at the mere thought.

"Of course you wouldn't." Mila gives me a warm stare, her eyes softening. "I'm sorry I followed you, Sam. I'm worried, that's all."

I give her a faint smile, my heart swelling with gratitude. "Don't be." My hold on her hand tightens, a silent plea. "Nik's perfectly good to me... And oh, so hot." My lips stretch into a malicious grin, heat rising in my cheeks.

Mila snickers, her eyes twinkling with mirth. "He is kind of hot."

I start, shocked by her phrasing. "Kind of?" My eyebrows shoot sky-high, my mouth falling open in mock offense. "How dare you?" I tease, a laugh bubbling up in my throat.

"Okay, he's super-hot," Mila concedes, her cheeks flushing pink.

"Damn right he is." I nod, choking back a laugh. "And we're going on a getaway this weekend." I take the golden spoon next to her cup and play with it in my hand, my heart skipping a beat at the thought of being alone with Nik.

My dear friend freezes, her eyes all but bulging out of their sockets. "You... what?" Poor thing, she can barely speak.

"He has a small house," I continue, dipping the spoon in the ice cream, the smooth, creamy texture making my mouth water. "And, guess where it is?"

"I don't know..." Mila mumbles, her voice cautious

and wary as she stares at me with undiluted apprehen-sion. "But I have a feeling you're gonna tell me."

I purse my lips and scoop a spoonful of gooey, sinful chocolate ice cream, my taste buds singing with delight. "In Brittany." My gaze cuts to hers, my eyes sparkling with glee and anticipation.

Mila releases a brief gasp, her hand flying to her mouth. "Samara, you're not seriously considering...?"

"I am," I tell her, my voice unwavering and more gleeful than she was when she ordered her velvety treat. Nik is infinitely superior to any Michelin-starred dessert. I'll eat him up in slow bites if I have to. The thought makes my heart sing, a warm, fuzzy feeling spreading through my chest.

"Can I count on your help?" I ask, my voice hopeful and pleading. "It's the only way it'll work."

"Sam..." Mila's voice is tormented, her face contorting with indecision.

"Please!" I beg her, my hands clasping together in front of me. "You wouldn't have to lie! You've been meaning to visit your sister anyway..."

Mila sucks at her teeth, her eyes darting between me and the ice cream. "Alright," she relents, her shoulders sagging in defeat.

I am beyond ecstatic, my heart soaring with joy. In one quick move, I sweep the glass off the table and pull Mila's ice cream towards me. "Let's order one more!" I say, dipping my spoon in the glass, the rich, decadent flavor exploding on my tongue. "My treat!"

Mila chortles a laugh, her eyes crinkling at the corners. "I told you... I knew you'd love it," she scolds me warmly, her voice tinged with affection.

"Yes, you did," I concede, a grin spreading across my face. "But then, you know me better than anyone, so it's hardly surprising." I wrinkle my nose and giggle, my heart light and carefree.

The next spoonful melts in my mouth, and I moan in delight, my eyes fluttering closed. "This is going to be the best weekend of my life," I say, my voice dreamy and wistful. "I know it. I can't wait for it to begin!"

And as I sit there, savoring the delicious ice cream and basking in the glow of Mila's friendship, I feel a sense of hope and excitement blooming in my chest. Come what may, I know that this weekend with Nik will be a turning point in our relationship, a chance to explore the depths of our feelings for each other.

And with Mila's support and understanding, I feel like anything is possible, like the whole world is at my fingertips.

I can't wait to see what the future holds.

15

NIK

A blur of memories flies past my mind as I meander through the mansion, our summer house, each room evoking a flicker of emotion, a fleeting glimpse of the warmth and nurturing times I spent here with my parents. I remember walking along the beach, the salty breeze whipping through my hair. I remember sitting by the fireplace, sipping hot cocoa on chilly evenings, the glow of the flames casting dancing shadows on the walls. But the details escape me, the moments fading like wisps of smoke, as if they belong to someone else's life.

It's been so long, my mother and father's features have all but faded. If not for a few framed photographs scattered in these rooms, I would have no recollection of my their faces whatsoever.

The air is cool, the rooms desolate despite Bram's

extensive renovations. He's stripped down the wallpaper, painted the walls, torn out the original floors and replaced them with modern hardwood. The changes are so drastic, it's like stepping into an entirely different place, one devoid of the comforting familiarity of my childhood. I can't even fathom the amount of money he's poured into this project, but I suppose it's better than him throwing it away on booze and parties, as he so often does.

November hits hard, and not just because of the wintry weather. Thirteen years ago, my parents died in this very house—a gas leak in the kitchen that wiped out the entire eastern wing. It was a miracle Bram and I survived, as well as my baby sister Clarissa, but the loss still aches like a fresh wound, the anniversary a painful reminder of all that we've lost.

I didn't even think about the significance of the date when I offered to bring Sam here, but now, as I stand in the foyer, I start to question the wisdom of my decision. But then I see her standing in the doorway, radiant in casual jeans and a cozy black sweater, her long tartan overcoat and cashmere scarf dangling from her arm. She's holding a small suitcase, and the sight of her chases away all my doubts and fears.

"Sam…!" I breathe, relief and joy washing over me as I dart to her side and pull her into my arms. My lips find hers, sealing them in a slow, fiery kiss that sets my soul ablaze. I feel her knees buckle against mine, and I can't stop the smile that tugs at the corner of my mouth, elated by her response. This was absolutely the right decision. I've longed to spend time alone with her, to have the freedom to be together without the weight of our families' expectations and prejudices bearing down on us.

Lazily, I part from her, my hand reaching up to tuck a stray lock of hair behind her ear. "You made it," I whisper, my voice rough with emotion.

"Gods," she sighs, her eyes wide with surprise. "What a welcome...!" She steps back, heading towards the doorway, a mischievous grin playing on her lips. "I'm just gonna step outside and walk in again, okay?"

I beam like a fool, but I don't care. She makes me feel like the happiest, luckiest man alive, and I wouldn't trade this moment for anything.

"No need," I murmur, taking her hand in mine and dragging her suitcase inside with the other. "We have the entire weekend ahead of us."

"Goodness..." Her eyes fly open, pleasure and anticipation dancing in their depths. "That we do."

"I was just going to start a fire. Want to come?" I suggest, beckoning her towards the living room.

Sam follows me, dropping onto the first sofa she sees with a contented sigh. While she rests, I crouch before the fireplace, laying kindling and logs with practiced ease. "This will burn beautifully," I mumble, my mind already lost in the mesmerizing dance of the flames.

"You seem to know what you're doing," she teases, rubbing her hands together for warmth.

I tear a newspaper into strips, carefully tucking them beneath the kindling. "I like fire," I tell her, throwing a playful glance over my shoulder. There's something about the primal power of the flames that calls to me, that soothes the restless ache in my soul.

I strike a match and toss it into the hearth, watching as the first tongues of fire lick at the logs, quickly growing into a roaring blaze. The heat washes over me, but it's nothing compared to the warmth that spreads through my chest at the sight of Sam, curled up on the sofa, watching me with soft eyes.

But as I stare into the flickering flames, something shifts inside me, a primal pull that I've never felt before. The fire seems to call to me, whispering secrets in a language that I don't understand, but that resonates deep within my soul. I find myself leaning closer, my eyes fixed on the dancing tongues of orange and red, the crackling of the logs fading into the background.

It's as if the world has fallen away, leaving nothing but the fire and the strange, insistent tugging in my chest. I feel a rush of power, of something ancient and wild stirring in my blood, and for a moment, I swear I can feel the heat of the flames on my skin, as if they're a part of me.

I don't know how long I sit there, transfixed by the flames, but gradually, I become aware of a voice calling my name,

"Nik?" she asks, a hint of concern in her voice. "Are you okay?"

Her gentle words pull me from my reverie, and I shift to face her, my heart skipping a beat at the sight of her beauty, more compelling than any flame.

"Yeah," I breathe, my voice rough with emotion.

"It's your birthday tomorrow," she says softly.

"Yeah..." I echo, and I blink in surprise before doing a double-take. "How do you know?"

The corner of her lips curls in a sly smile. "You think you're the only one with a computer?" she replies, shrugging her shoulders.

"Huh..." I utter, pushing myself to my feet and crossing to the sofa. "So, you've been looking me up?" My tone is deliberately enticing, my eyebrow raised in a silent challenge.

"Yeah," she says, mirroring my usual straight answers. "No wife. No kids... You're good."

I snicker, sinking down beside her, our thighs brushing. It feels right, being here with her, the ease and honesty between us a balm to my battered soul. We wear no masks, pretend to be nothing other than what we are. And it works, this delicate balance we've found.

"I thought you would've had plans for your birthday," she continues, smoothing her hands over her toned thighs, the gesture sending a shiver down my spine.

My gaze roves over her, drinking in every sensual curve, every delicate feature, until it settles on her eyes, twin pools of molten garnet, glittering with magic and promise. "I do," I whisper, my voice low and rough.

She starts, her expression slackening for an instant. "Oh?" she breathes, her eyebrows lifting in surprise.

"Being with you," I confess, my heart laid bare. "I can't think of a better way to spend my birthday weekend."

A blush stains her cheeks, and I lean in, capturing her lips in a heartfelt kiss that steals my breath and sets my blood on fire. She kisses me back with equal fervor, and my heart soars, a dizzying sense of rightness settling over me.

When we part, I search her face, my curiosity getting the better of me. "How did you do it?" I ask, my brow furrowed.

"Do what?" she says, confusion clouding her features.

"How did you manage to come here without getting into trouble with the Ursa clan?" I clarify, genuinely intrigued. The last time I set foot in Sam's house, the place was swarming with guards, a common sight for men in Gavriil's position, or my brother's.

"Oh, that." She shoots up her eyebrows, a sly smile

tugging at her lips. "Well," she sighs, "remember my friend Mila?"

I crack a smile, the memory of our interrupted tryst still fresh in my mind. "How could I forget?"

Her cheeks flush again, and the sight steals my breath, my heart skipping a beat. "Her sister lives here," she explains. "I told Gavriil I'd come with Mila and spend a few days in town."

"Ah..." I utter, throwing her a knowing look. "So, you lied." The thought of her deceiving her brother, the mighty Ursa King, sends a thrill through me, a rush of excitement at her daring.

"I did not," she retorts instantly, a delicious pout on her lips. "I specifically told my brother I'd come here with Mila, not that I'd *stay* with her."

I tilt my head, watching her with undisguised delight, my heart swelling with affection at the adorable way her nose wrinkles, the mischief dancing in her eyes. "Do you want to go for a walk on the beach?" I ask, hope blossoming in my chest.

"I thought you'd never ask," she says, her smile brighter than the sun.

My fingers lace with hers, a perfect fit, as we rise from the sofa, ready to face whatever the future may hold, as long as we're together. The weight of the past, the ghosts that haunt this house, fade away in the warmth of her presence, replaced by a sense of peace and rightness that I've never known before.

With Sam by my side, I feel like I can take on the world, like anything is possible. And as we step out into the crisp November air, the sound of the waves crashing against the shore a soothing melody, I know that this birthday, this weekend, will be one I'll never forget.

16

NIK

The winter sun bleeds its dying rays behind us as we stroll along the beach, the sand cool and soft beneath our feet. It's a peaceful start to the evening, the shoreline deserted save for the two of us. We walk in silence, enjoying each other's company, the quiet intimacy of the moment. It's just the way I dreamed it would be, time seeming to fly by when I'm with Sam.

We stop by the rocks, settling down to contemplate the dusky horizon. The chilly breeze picks up, tangling Sam's dark locks and brushing them against her smooth cheeks. I watch, transfixed, my heart swelling with a rush of emotion that I can't quite name.

"It's a lovely home you have here," she says, her voice soft and contemplative.

I glide an inch closer to her, careful to leave enough

distance between us, not wanting to overwhelm her with the intensity of my feelings. But gods, do I long to close that gap, to pull her into my arms and never let go.

"It belonged to my grandparents," I explain, forcing myself to focus on the conversation at hand. "It later passed on to my mother, and now to us—to my brother Bram, I should say."

She pulls back her hair, tying it into a high, messy bun that only serves to highlight the delicate lines of her face. When she turns to me, her eyes are luminous in the fading light. "Do you ever stop to think of it?" she asks, a delicious frown creasing her brow.

I can't help but smile, intrigued by the question. "Think of what?" I murmur, my gaze fixed on her face.

"How our brothers have shaped our entire existence," she elaborates, turning back to the sea. Her profile gleams, kissed by the last rays of daylight, and I find myself breathless at the sight. "We live in the shadows of powerful leaders."

"Mm..." I utter, resting my arms on my knees as I ponder her words. It's a heavy topic, one that I wasn't expecting, but I find myself drawn to the depths of her mind, the way she sees the world.

"I don't mind it," she continues, hugging her knees to her chest. "Living in shadows."

I inch closer, my arm brushing against hers, and the sudden thrill of contact makes my breath hitch. I force myself to speak past the lump in my throat. "Me neither. I'd even go so far as to say it plays to my advantage," I whisper, my gaze drifting to the darkening ocean. I take a deep breath, the salty air filling my lungs, grounding me in the moment.

"Really?" she asks, turning to face me once more. "In what way?"

Will I ever stop feeling this sudden restlessness when our eyes meet? I hope not. "Nobody cares to know what I do or why..." I pause, trying to steady my racing heart. "I grew up free from any expectations, but I missed being home."

"Oh, that's right," she says, understanding dawning in her eyes. "You were sent away."

Her words are blunt, but not unkind, and I appreciate her honesty. "I guess that's hardly a secret nowadays." I shrug, trying to play off the old hurt. "Yeah, Bram sent me off to boarding school. A little over ten years ago."

"Gavriil became king around that time..." she muses, her brow furrowing in thought. "It was that way for me too, you know. Losing my parents, growing up under my brother's guardianship—not the boarding school part."

"I'm glad you skipped living that part," I mumble, unable to keep the bitterness from my voice.

Her expression shifts, lightness giving way to grave concern as her maroon eyes bore into mine. "You have every reason to resent Bram," she tells me, her voice soft but fierce. "I know I would have, had I been displaced from my home."

"Yeah, well..." I straighten, a familiar pain pulsing in my temples. The headache is back, hitting me with no warning, threatening to ruin this perfect moment. I wince, unable to hide my discomfort.

"Nik? What is it?" Sam asks, her hand smoothing over mine, the touch sending sparks racing through my veins. "Is it something I said?"

Gods, not now. Why did it have to happen now, of all times? "No, not at all," I assure her. "It's this headache..." I groan, pressing a hand to my temple, trying to will the pain away.

"We should head back," Sam suggests, rising to her feet. "Maybe we should start thinking about dinner."

I stand, mirroring her posture, the movement sending a fresh wave of agony through my skull. "Yeah, that must be it..." I say, trying to keep my voice steady.

But it's not. I know full well that the pain won't go away, not for a while at least. I've been getting these headaches on and off for months now, each one worse than the last. I wish to all the gods that it would disappear, that I could enjoy this precious time with Sam without the shadow of my own body betraying me.

We make the walk back to the house in silence, the pain throbbing behind my eyes with every step. I curse myself for spoiling our first evening together, for not being stronger, better.

Just perfect.

As we enter the house, I try to push aside the guilt and frustration, focusing instead on the simple task of finding my medication. But with each passing moment, the pain seems to intensify, a searing, white-hot agony that threatens to split my skull in two.

I stumble into the kitchen, my vision blurring at the edges as I frantically search for the familiar prescription bottle. I can feel Sam's concerned gaze on me, but I can't bring myself to meet her eyes, too ashamed of my own weakness.

I hate relying on medication, don't like the idea of chemicals messing with my body. But after months of trying every natural remedy under the sun, I've come to accept that the drugs are the only thing that can stop the pain.

A low growl rumbles in my chest as I search, frustration mounting with each passing second. "Dammit, where are they?" I mutter under my breath.

I clench my jaw, fighting back the scream that threatens to tear from my throat. I can't let Sam see me like this, can't let her witness the depths of my flaws. She deserves better than this, better than a man who can't even make it through a single evening without being brought to his knees by his own treacherous body.

And then, through the haze of agony, I hear Sam's

voice, soft and gentle, like a soothing balm on my battered soul. "Are these your pills?" she asks, and I could weep with relief.

I look up to see her holding the prescription bottle, and instant ease washes over me. "Yeah," I manage, taking the bottle from her hand. If this fucking headache doesn't go away soon, I know my mood will only sour further. And I don't want that, not tonight, not when she's here with me. "Thanks." It's all I can muster, but I hope she can hear the gratitude in my voice.

I pull off the cap and slip a couple of pills under my tongue, the bitter taste making me grimace. The drugs dissolve instantly, but I know the relief won't be as immediate. Twenty minutes, the doctor said. It seems like an eternity when the pain is this intense, this all-consuming.

And the headaches seem to be getting worse each time, the agony more unbearable, the duration longer. My pulse quickens at the thought, a flicker of fear igniting in my gut. Maybe it's just my imagination, my mind playing tricks on me.

I force myself to focus on Sam, on the way she's watching me with those beautiful, concerned eyes. She's here, with me, and that's all that matters.

I step closer, my hand smoothing along her supple arm, unable to resist the urge to touch her. "Listen, I'm really sorry about this..." I say, my voice rough with pain and regret.

"No, don't say that," she soothes, and I can tell she means it, that she understands. "Do you want to eat something?" Her voice is sweet as honey.

But the thought of food makes my stomach turn, the nausea that always accompanies these headaches rearing its ugly head. "I think I'll just lie down for a while..." I say, trying to keep my tone light, nonchalant. "If you don't mind."

"Not at all." Sam bites her lower lip, the gesture so tempting that it takes all my willpower not to pull her into my arms and kiss her senseless. "A good night's rest is all you need."

I nod, reluctant to leave her, but knowing that I'm in no state to be good company right now. "What about you?" I ask, not wanting her to feel neglected, abandoned.

She snickers, the sound like music to my ears. "Oh, I'm definitely eating something." Her lips stretch into a smile. And gods, she's never been more beautiful. "I'm hungry as hell."

A laugh bursts from my chest, the sound surprising me. Even in the midst of my pain, she can still make me smile, can still bring light to my darkness. "Sounds like a solid plan," I tell her, stepping back towards the threshold, my body heavy with exhaustion. "I'll see you tomorrow then."

"Good night," she says, already pulling open the fridge, her appetite apparently unaffected by my ailment. I guess she wasn't kidding when she said she was hungry.

I make my way to the bedroom, each step an effort, the pain throbbing in time with my heartbeat. As I collapse onto the bed, I send up a silent prayer to any god who might be listening.

Please, let this pass. Let me be whole and healthy again, so that I can be the man that Sam deserves, the man that I want to be.

But even as I drift off into a restless sleep, the pain chasing me into my dreams, I can't shake the feeling that something is changing within me, that these headaches are more than just a physical ailment.

There's a darkness lurking beneath the surface, a shadow that grows with each passing day. And I fear that one day, it will consume me entirely, leaving nothing but ashes in its wake—the nonsensical ramblings of a mind in the grip of a powerful stupor.

17

SAM

As Nik leaves the kitchen, I'm already rummaging through the fridge, my stomach churning with hunger. I don't even wait for him to disappear from view before I'm pulling open drawers and cabinets, my eyes widening at the array of fresh, vibrant fruits and vegetables that greet me. It's an impressive sight, one that speaks to Nik's healthy lifestyle.

I open the freezer, hoping to find something quick and easy to satisfy my cravings. Instead, I'm met with a dozen healthy-looking smoothies, each one a different color and no doubt packed with nutrients. I wrinkle my nose, my appetite demanding something more substantial.

And then I see the meat. Venison, beef, lamb

chops... It's enough to make my mouth water, and I can't help but wonder who would win in a contest between Gavriil's freezer and Nik's. It's a close call, but I have a feeling Nik might just edge out my brother in terms of sheer variety.

"Maybe I should give the shakes a try..." I muse, tilting my head as I consider the options before me. But even as the words leave my mouth, I know it's a lost cause. I'm not in the mood for a green juice, no matter how healthy it might be.

With a sigh, I shut the drawer and pull out a block of cheese and what looks like a fancy roasted turkey breast. There's some bread on the island, and I know instantly what I'm going to make.

"A regular sandwich it is," I mumble to myself, my stomach grumbling in anticipation. "No green juice for me."

But as I stare at the ingredients laid out before me, a sudden thought pierces through the haze of hunger. Mila's words, spoken just hours before, echo in my mind, and I feel a chill run down my spine.

"Nikolaas Draken is a killer."

I try to shake off the unease, but it clings to me like a second skin. It's ridiculous, I tell myself. Nik is no killer, no matter what Mila or anyone else might say. He's kind and gentle, with a heart as big as the ocean. He would never do something so heinous, so cruel.

And yet, as I reach for a knife to slice the bread, I find myself hesitating. A voice in my head, one that sounds suspiciously like my own, whispers its doubts.

You should make sure you're safe. Just in case.

I feel a flicker of shame at the thought, at the idea that I could ever doubt Nik's intentions. But I can't help myself. Slowly, cautiously, I pull open the island's drawer, my eyes scanning its contents.

Forks, spoons, and other silverware greet me, but no knives. Where are all the knives?

My heart begins to race, my palms growing damp with sweat. I open a cabinet, my movements jerky and uncoordinated, and finally glimpse the knife block tucked away in the back.

"Gods, Brenda! Stop it!" I stammer, my voice echoing in the empty kitchen. I feel like a fool, talking to my own conscience like some kind of madwoman.

But even as I berate myself, I can't shake the nagging sense of unease. It's not like Nik to be so secretive, to hide something as innocuous as a knife block. What could he be trying to conceal?

I take a deep breath, trying to calm my racing thoughts. Of course, Nik isn't a killer. Those are Gavriil's words, spoken in the heat of the moment, fueled by centuries of hatred and mistrust. The boy I know, the one I've come to care for so deeply, is sweet and harmless. He would never do something as heinous as taking a life.

My brother, on the other hand... He's already killed his fair share of bears, starting with the one who took his beloved mate, Luciana. The thought of him keeping the poor creature's fur draped over the library chair makes me shudder, revulsion and horror twisting in my gut.

I finish making my sandwich, wrapping it in a napkin with shaking hands. Now that Nik has gone to bed, I take my time wandering through the rooms, nibbling at my dinner as I go.

Maybe I'll be able to glean some new insight into the man I'm falling for, some clue to the secrets he keeps locked away. But even as I search, I know it's a futile effort. Nik has been straightforward from the start, his honesty and openness one of the things I love most about him. He wears no masks, hides behind no pretenses.

As I enter the parlor, my sandwich nothing more than a few stray crumbs, I spot a couple of picture frames on the mantelpiece. Curiosity gets the better of me, and I move closer, my eyes widening as I take in the sight before me.

As I study the photograph, my eyes are drawn to the two young boys standing in front of a gorgeous couple. Their faces are alight with joy and laughter, their grins wide and carefree. The man and woman behind them are clearly their parents, the resemblance unmistakable.

But it's the little girl cradled in her mother's arms

that catches my attention. She's just a baby, her face round and sweet, her eyes wide and curious. I recognize her instantly, even though she's much younger in this picture.

Clarissa. Nik's baby sister, the one I met at the seance just a few short weeks ago.

She had been quiet and reserved then, her eyes shadowed with a grief that seemed too heavy for someone so young. But here, in this frozen moment of time, she is all smiles and giggles, her tiny hands reaching out to grasp at her brother's hair.

I trace the familiar lines of Nik's nose, the curve of his lips, and feel a pang of sorrow in my chest. He looks so happy here, so carefree and unburdened. It's a stark contrast to the man I know now, the one who carries the weight of the world on his shoulders.

I wonder what it must have been like for him, losing his parents at such a young age. And not just him, but Clarissa too. She would have been just a baby when they died, too young to even remember their faces or the sound of their voices.

My heart aches for them both, for the childhood they never got to have, for the love and guidance they were so cruelly denied. I think of my own parents, of the hole their loss has left in my life, and I feel a kinship with Nik and Clarissa that goes beyond mere friendship or attraction.

The pain of that loss, the ache of that absence, is something I know all too well. Life can be so cruel, so unfair, to take away the people we love most just when we need them the most.

We are all survivors, all of us who have lost and grieved and somehow found the strength to carry on. It's a bond that can never be broken, a shared experience that ties us together in ways that words can never fully express.

As I stare at the picture, at the smiling faces of a family long gone, I make a silent vow. I will be there for Nik. I will stand by his side and help him carry the burden of his loss.

Because that's what family does. That's what love is all about.

I yawn, the events of the day finally catching up with me. Nik never mentioned where my room was, but I'm too tired to go searching for him now. I'll just follow the staircase and find my suitcase. That's where my room must be.

As I climb the stairs, my mind is a whirlwind of thoughts and emotions. The doubts that plagued me in the kitchen have faded, replaced by a sense of warmth and affection for the man who has opened his home and his heart to me.

As I drift off to sleep, I know, with a certainty that goes beyond reason or logic, that Nik is not the monster my brother and the rest of the Ursa clan would paint him to be. He is good and kind and true, and I am lucky to have found him.

For now, that is all I need to know.

18

SAM

I'm lying in bed, gazing at the starry evening sky before me, a glittering canvas hanging above the darkened ocean. The sound of waves crashing against the shore wraps me in a cocoon of pure delight, the gentle rhythm soothing my restless mind. The room itself is like something out of a magazine, a Presidential Suite in a luxurious hotel, with tall ceilings, a spacious parlor, and breathtaking panoramic windows.

It feels like a dream to be here, in this moment, with Nik just a heartbeat away. I know sleep will be elusive tonight, my thoughts too full of him, of the connection that simmers between us.

A pang of regret tugs at my heart as I think back to our early night, the way Nik's headache forced us to cut our evening short. Even through the pain, he managed to keep a smile on his face, his mood towards me as sweet as ever. And the fact that he hadn't assumed we'd share a room? It only made me fall for him harder.

I had thought, at first, that this might be a one-night thing. A chance to get Nik out of my system, to scratch an itch and move on. But the more time I spend with him, the more I feel myself letting go of my old fears, my old defenses. The truth is, I'm falling hard and fast for this man, and there's no denying the invisible pull between us, a force that feels almost like magic.

The creak of the door jolts me from my thoughts, and I turn my head to see Nik's tall, well-built silhouette standing in the doorway, his broad shoulders and muscular torso etched in the twilight.

My heart stutters in my chest, my pulse skyrocketing as a million thoughts race through my mind. What is he doing here? What does this mean? I part my lips, trying to find the words, but nothing comes out.

As Nik enters the room, his body catches the slanted beams of moonlight that pierce through the glass, highlighting every toned muscle, every inch of his perfect form. He's wearing nothing but sleek boxer briefs, the fabric clinging to his powerful thighs, and I feel a rush of heat flood through me at the sight.

My eyes are drawn to the dragon inked across his chest, the intricate design curling around his arm and shoulder. His clan's sigil, a mark of his heritage, his power. And lower still, to the eight-pack that carves his abs, the taut expanse of flesh that disappears beneath the waistband of his briefs.

When I finally meet his gaze, I'm struck by the intensity I see there, his ice-blue eyes glinting in the shadows like sparkling sapphires. They're fierce and full of desire as they rove over my bare legs, gliding up my body's every curve, devouring me without even laying a finger on me.

Nik moves closer, his steps silent and predatory, until he stops at the foot of the bed. My breath hitches in my throat, my heart pounding so hard I'm sure he can hear it. What is he going to do? I can barely breathe, my mind spinning with possibilities.

He lays his hands on the mattress, his muscled back slightly crouched as he climbs onto the bed with the graceful stealth of a tiger. In an instant, I'm trapped beneath his lustful stare, my body frozen, my mind reeling. Is this real, or am I dreaming?

His face draws close to mine, his calloused hand cupping the side of my face with a tenderness that makes my heart ache. And then his lips are on my skin, tracing a path of searing kisses along the curve of my shoulder, up the column of my neck. Every inch of my body comes alive at his touch, tingling with desire and need.

This is real. This is happening.

Nik's fingers make quick work of the buttons on my pajama top, his touch igniting a fire in my veins. I want him, need him, with an urgency that takes my breath away. It feels like an eternity of foreplay has passed since our first kiss, and I don't think I can wait any longer.

I reach up to tug his mouth to mine, desperate to taste him, to lose myself in his kiss. But in a flash, he seizes my wrist and pins it above my head, trapping me beneath the weight of his body, his muscular chest pressing against mine. Without a word, his mouth trails lower, tormenting me with searing kisses that travel down my collarbone to the valley between my breasts.

I catch my panting breath, his intoxicating cologne filling my lungs, soothing my racing heart. But it's a fleeting respite, my body already aching for more.

A moan slips from my lips as his free hand smooths down my hip, finding its way between my thighs. I'm on fire for him, every nerve ending sparking with need. Memories of that night at the club flash through my mind, the way he touched me, the way he made me feel. I want that again, want him, more than I've ever wanted anything in my life.

Our clothes are shed in a frenzy of desperate hands and seeking mouths. Nik's lips trail lower, his kisses searing a path down my belly, until they reach the apex of my thighs. I writhe and moan beneath his touch, his powerful hold on me only heightening my pleasure.

He smiles against my skin, his caress growing bolder, more demanding, until I'm teetering on the brink of ecstasy. Once, and then again, he pushes me over the edge, my body convulsing with the force of my release. "Oh, gods!" I cry out, breathless and elated. "Nik!" I can't wait any longer. I need him now, or I'm going to combust.

He straightens, watching me with hungry eyes as I come down from my high. And then his body is lowering over mine, his lips sealing over my own in a kiss that steals my breath and sets my soul on fire. I moan into his mouth, my tongue tangling with his in a dance of passion and need.

"Nik..." I beg again, my hand cupping his square jaw, my fingers tracing the stubble that roughens his skin.

A low growl rumbles in his chest, and he grips my wrists roughly, pinning both of my hands above my head. I'm left panting, my chest heaving, my body aching for his touch.

"Are you ready for me?" he purrs, his voice a seductive rumble that sends shivers down my spine.

"Uh-huh..." I breathe, my mind hazy with desire.

When his hardness slips between my thighs, I moan, my body writhing beneath his. And then he's sheathing himself inside me, filling me so completely that I gasp at the sweet agony of it.

"Good girl..." he sighs in my ear, the words shooting a thrill straight to my core. "Take every... fucking... inch." He thrusts deeper, stretching me in ways that make me see stars. I bite my lip, my eyes squeezing shut at the exquisite fullness that consumes me. He's so big, so deep, it feels as if he touches every part of me—body, mind, and soul.

Nik's thrusts are slow and deliberate at first, as if he's savoring every inch he takes, every moan that escapes my lips. His hands now cradle my hips, holding me steady as he plunges deeper and deeper within me, his manhood sliding against nerve endings I didn't know existed. The intensity of the sensation is almost too much to bear, yet I don't want it to end.

My body molds to his, every curve and plane fitting together like puzzle pieces. In his arms, I feel free, feel home, like I've finally found the place I belong. Our bodies rock together in perfect harmony, the pleasure building and building until I'm lost in a haze of sensation.

My nails dig into the bedding, and I arch my back to meet his every thrust, desperate for more. He's primal now, a dragon claiming his mate, and I'm powerless to resist. The night air swirls around us, whirling with our mingled scents: his earthy cologne and my feminine musk.

"You feel so good," he groans against my ear, his voice raw with need. "So wet sánd tight." And then he kisses down my neck, lavishing hot, open-mouthed kisses on my collarbone that send shivers of pleasure through me. His hands roam my body, molding and squeezing each curve of my heated flesh as if he's memorizing every inch of me.

He picks up the pace, driving into me with more force, and I gasp at the sheer intensity of it all. "Nik... oh, gods... yes!" I moan unabashedly, suffused in the heady pleasure of it all. My senses are on fire, every nerve ending alive with sensation as our bodies dance together in sublime unison.

"That's it... so good..." he groans in response, his breath hot against my ear. His grip on my wrists tightens, but the pain only heightens the pleasure coursing through my veins. "You're mine."

He growls as he pushes deeper, the primal sound making my toes curl. "Mine," he repeats, his voice guttural and feral, "I've been yours from the start, and now you're mine."

The way he says it, like it's a fact, like it's the only truth there ever was, shoots a thrill through my veins. He pulls out only to slam back in again with a force that makes the bedframe shake, and I cry out his name. Gods, it feels so good. So right.

His lips find my breast, sucking on the sensitive skin until I'm whimpering under him. His hands roam my body, leaving a trail of fire in their wake as he squeezes my hips, the contact only heightening the ecstasy coursing through me.

"Oh, gods... Nik..."

He picks up the pace even more, his thrusts harder

and deeper now, and I can feel myself teetering on the edge again. Bright colors flash before my eyes as the orgasm builds inside me like a storm gathering in the distance.

"You look so good… lying there and taking it," he purrs against my ear.

His words fan the flames of my desire, and I buck my hips against his, desperate for more. "Nik… harder," I pant, lost in the sensation of him deep inside me. His pace increases, and our bodies collide with a breathtaking force that sets every nerve ending ablaze.

"Yes… like that," I moan, my back arching in ecstasy.

He obliges, his movements becoming even more frenzied as he plunges into me with a primal urgency that sends shocks of ecstasy through my very core. The room is filled with our mingled scents: his musky cologne and my heady arousal, blending to create something entirely our own.

"Oh, gods… I'm so close," I gasp, nails digging into the sheets as the pleasure builds within me like a storm about to break loose. Sweat sheens on my skin, mingling with the perspiration on his as our bodies move as one. He groans in response, his breathing ragged and uneven in my ear.

"That's it… give in for me… let go for me," Nik commands between sultry kisses along my collarbone.

"Nik… I can't… I can't… ah!" I pant, my breathing

ragged as the pleasure mounts. I'm so close, and he knows it. He traces a line of kisses along my inner thigh, sending goosebumps erupting on my skin. His hands explore my body with a newfound fervor, squeezing and kneading the taut flesh of my hips and buttocks as if he's trying to memorize every inch of me.

"Come for me, Sam," he growls against my ear, his voice a deep, primal rumble that shoots straight to my core. "Give it all to me."

With those words, the dam breaks. My climax surges through me in bright, pulsing waves of ecstasy, and I cry out his name as my body shakes and quivers beneath his. My nails dig into his shoulders, grazing his skin as I arch my back in surrender.

Nik doesn't stop there, however. He pulls me even closer to him, if that were even possible, and thrusts even deeper and harder as he follows me over the edge. "You're mine," he growls against my neck, his voice thick with passion as he claims me in more ways than one. "Now… and forever."

The room around us is a blur of colors and shadows, the only thing in focus being the rise and fall of our chests as we catch our breaths. Nik gently rolls us over, so I'm lying on my back, and he leans over me, his eyes locked with mine. Sweat glistening on both our brows, we share a moment of raw intimacy that goes beyond the physical.

His lips part to speak, but hesitation makes him

purse them shut again. Then finally, the words escape him. "That was amazing," he whispers, his voice hoarse from our passionate lovemaking but laced with raw emotion. "*You* are fucking amazing."

I smile up at him, my heart swelling with warmth as I trace my finger along his jawline. "You're *fucking amazing* too," I reply, feeling the heat rise to my cheeks.

We share a quiet laugh, and he pulls me into his arms. Our breathing evens out, our hearts slowing to their normal rhythms. We stay entangled in each other's arms. I gently lay my head over his chest, listening to his quickened heartbeat—that's when I start to feel it.

"Nik..." I murmur, my voice soft in the quiet room.

"Yeah?" he replies, his fingers tracing idle patterns on my shoulder.

"You're so hot," I tell him, hoping he can hear the worry in my voice.

He snickers, the sound pleased and a little smug. "You're *hot* too..."

The frown on my face deepens. "No, that's not what I mean," I say, lifting my head to look at him. "You're burning up!"

We both stare at his chest, shocked to see his skin gleaming a vivid red. Patches of flesh subtly blush and coalesce into larger, incandescent plaques, like burning coals smoldering beneath the surface.

"What the...?" Nik springs up on the bed, his eyes wide with alarm as he takes in the sight of his arms, glowing with a muted crimson light that seems to come from within.

My brow furrows as I study him, my mind racing with possibilities. "I've never seen anything like it..." I murmur, speaking as a witch. And when his eyes meet mine, I can tell he understands the significance of my words.

I lean closer, sweeping a hand over his forehead, feeling the heat that radiates from his skin. "How do you feel?" I ask, my voice tight with concern. His cheeks are flushed, his face warm to the touch. I think he might be running a fever.

"I feel perfectly fine," he says, but I can hear the unease in his voice, the fear that lurks beneath the surface.

"Not warm or chilly?" I press, needing to know more.

"Slightly warm, yeah." Nik's chest heaves with each rapid breath, his heart racing beneath my palm.

Oh, gods... Oh, no.

Without another word, I reach over and turn on the light, needing to see him more clearly. Nik winces and tries to shy away, but I straddle his waist, cradling his face in my hands.

"Let me see," I whisper, my voice soothing and gentle. He jerks back, but I hold firm. "*Please.*"

Slowly, reluctantly, he opens his eyes. His pupils are dilated, pools of fathomless darkness. And when the light hits them, they constrict into thin, slitted lines.

In that moment, I know.

A sharp breath leaves my lungs, my heart clenching in my chest.

Nik covers my hands with his own, leaning forward, his eyes searching mine. "What is it?" he asks, the worry in his voice almost tangible.

"I've seen this before..." I breathe, the words sticking in my throat. "Something similar, at least."

For the first time since I've known him, Nik's confidence wavers, a flicker of fear crossing his face. "When?"

"My brother's first shift," I say, the air freezing in my lungs.

"No," he growls, his expression hardening, his jaw clenching tight. "No. That's impossible. There hasn't been a dragon shifter in the family for three hundred years..."

But I know what I saw, know the signs that can't be ignored. "I think there is now," I say softly, my gaze never leaving his.

"No! You're wrong!" Nik leaps from the bed, grabbing his boxers and pulling them on with jerky, agitated movements.

My eyes shutter closed for a moment, my mind whirling with everything I've ever learned about magic, trying to make sense of the impossible. "The headaches," I begin, my voice low and steady. "The temperature spikes, the spell that fire casts over you…" I open my eyes, meeting his gaze head-on. "My brother first shifted when he turned sixteen. I guess dragons shift at twenty-one."

"What?" Nik stares at me, his eyes wide with shock and disbelief.

"Your birthday…" I murmur, the pieces clicking into place. "It's a few hours away." I swallow hard, the tension between us thick and heavy.

"Sam, what are you saying?" His voice is rough, edged with desperation.

A chill silence fills the room, the weight of my next words hanging in the air.

"I think you'll turn into a dragon tomorrow."

19

NIK

I can all but feel the color draining from my face, my expression slackening as the full weight of Sam's words hits me like a physical blow.

Fuck.

My world is shattering, the ground crumbling beneath my feet. Sam doesn't tiptoe around the issue, her words ruthless and uncompromising, spoken with the sheer conviction that only the fiercest of witches can muster.

The worst part is, it makes sense. I've heard about the symptoms that precede the first shift in wolves and bears, the signs that herald the awakening of their inner beasts. Why would a dragon's be any different? My recent headaches, the dizziness, the blurred vision... it all adds up, clicking into place like the pieces of a horrifying puzzle. And above all else, I trust

Samara's judgment, her skill as a witch beyond reproach.

The realization hits me hard, a tidal wave of fear and desperation crashing over me. Just moments ago, as we lay tangled in the aftermath of our lovemaking, I thought I'd known true fear for the first time. The words had been there, on the tip of my tongue, three simple syllables that held the power to change everything between us: *I love you.*

But I swallowed them back, too frightened of scaring her away, of losing the precious connection we have forged. I had thought that nothing could be more terrifying than the prospect of baring my soul to her, of laying my heart at her feet and praying that she would cherish it.

I was wrong.

Because now, faced with the possibility of shifting into a dragon, of becoming a creature of myth and legend, my earlier fears seem laughably trivial. But it's not my own safety that concerns me, not my own well-being that sends icy tendrils of dread curling through my veins.

No, it's the thought of hurting Sam, of losing control and becoming a danger to the woman I love... that's the true nightmare made real. The idea of my claws rending her flesh, my fangs sinking into her soft skin... it's enough to make me want to howl with despair, to fall to my knees and beg whatever gods might be listening to spare her from my own monstrosity.

I'd been afraid to tell her I loved her, afraid that three little words might shatter the delicate balance between us. But now, I would give anything to go back to that moment, to hold her in my arms and whisper my devotion against her skin, to make sure she knows the depth and breadth of my feelings for her.

Because if tomorrow brings the horror that Sam predicts, if I do shift into a creature of smoke and flame and fury... everything will change. This isn't an ordinary wolf or a bear we're talking about, but a true fire-breather as the world has not seen in centuries.

I must protect her—from myself.

The thought is a blade to the heart, a pain so sharp and acute that it steals my breath and brings hot tears to my eyes. Because I can't lose her, can't bear the thought of a world without her in it. In just a few short weeks, she's become everything to me—my reason for being, the guiding light that leads me home.

And still, I'm not willing to risk her life so recklessly. Not on a whim of selfishness. So I cling to her now, my arms banded tight around her waist, my face buried in the crook of her neck as I breathe in the sweet, familiar scent of her. I let her love wash over me, let it soothe the jagged edges of my fear.

My gaze cuts to her, my heart clenching at the sight of her beautiful face, the concern and love that shines in her eyes. "You gotta go," I tell her, the words tearing at my throat, my soul. But there's no way around this, no other choice to make. Not now.

Sam jumps to her knees on the bed, her brow furrowing in a fierce scowl. "What did you say?" she demands, glaring at me with a mix of hurt and indignation. She's a feisty little bear, *my* little bear, and the thought of pushing her away is like a knife to the heart.

"No!" She pouts, slipping into her oversized pajama top with jerky, agitated movements. "Nik, I'm not leaving you alone!"

My breath catches in my throat, my lungs constricting with the force of my fear. "If I..." I stop, forcing myself to make peace with this shattering truth, to accept the inevitable. "*When* I shift into a dragon, I don't think I'll know who you are." The words are like ashes on my tongue, bitter and choking. The thought of losing myself, of becoming a mindless beast with no memory of the woman I adore... it makes me shudder with revulsion and terror.

Sam bites her lower lip, her gaze drifting as she considers my words. "Yeah, that might happen..." she admits softly, her voice tinged with a sadness that breaks my heart. "It takes time for a shifter to tame its beast." But then she's facing me again, her eyes alight with a fierce determination that takes my breath away. "I won't leave you."

Tears rim my eyes, fear and anxiety warring in my

chest until I feel like I can't breathe, can't think beyond the panic that claws at my mind. It's too much, too fast, and I feel like I'm drowning in a sea of my own help-lessness.

"Sam..." I choke out, my lips pursing as I drop to my knees, burying my face in my hands. For the first time in longer than I can remember, I weep, hot tears spilling down my cheeks as sobs wrack my body.

And then she's there, her delicate hands smoothing over my jawline, her touch a balm to my battered soul. She kneels before me, her eyes searching mine until our gazes lock, hers full of unwavering resolve and undiluted love, mine brimming with dread and uncertainty.

"I'm here, Nik..." she whispers, her voice a lifeline in the darkness. "I'm not going anywhere."

On an impulse born of desperation and love, I wrap my arms around her waist and pull her to me, burying my face in the crook of her shoulder. Her fingers glide through my hair, her touch soothing and gentle as she draws me closer, peppering my cheeks, my nose, my lips with soft kisses that chase away the shadows of my fear.

This is a first for me—this vulnerability, this open-ness. I've never let anyone see me like this, never allowed myself to be weak or afraid in front of another person. But with Sam, it feels right, feels safe in a way that I've never known before.

For once, I don't feel alone. I feel loved, cherished, accepted for all that I am and all that I may become.

And as I cling to her, my face wet with tears and my heart full to bursting, I know that whatever tomorrow brings, whatever challenges we may face, we'll face them together.

Because that's what love is, in the end. It's the willingness to stand by someone's side, to weather the storms and face the darkness, no matter what. And as I hold Sam in my arms, I know that I've found that kind of love, the kind that lasts a lifetime.

Come what may, we'll find a way through this.

20

NIK

I overslept. When I open my eyes, the space beside me is empty, the sheets still warm with the memory of Sam's body. Sunlight glares through the bay windows, filling the white room with a radiance that borders on painful. Last night, we fell asleep in each other's arms, her presence a balm to my troubled soul, filling my heart with an inexplicable sense of peace. Is this what it feels like to have found my mate?

It is.

Sluggishly, I rise from the bed, reality crashing over me with each blundering step towards the shower. As the cool water pours over my head and trickles down my face, I try to come to terms with the truth. This is who I am, who I'm meant to be, no matter what happens. The blood of the dragon lineage courses through my veins, a legacy I can no longer deny.

As I brush my teeth, I notice a subtle difference in my reflection. Leaning closer to the mirror, I bare my teeth, my eyes widening at the sight of pointy fangs. Fear and uncertainty churn in my gut. I don't know what's going to happen. I'm flying blind into uncharted territory. But as I head downstairs, I cling to the one conviction that anchors me: this is my destiny, my birthright.

Gods, it's so late. Sam let me sleep in, a gesture that fills me with warmth and gratitude. She's amazing, a true wonder. I can't imagine anyone else standing by my side after learning that their boyfriend is about to turn into a fire-breathing beast. But Sam's not the type to run from a challenge. I should have known that from the moment I saw her smash that bottle at the nightclub.

A smile curls my lips at the memory, a snicker escaping me as I shake my head. Fuck, I love her. It's as simple and profound as that. I love her with every fiber of my being, with a depth and intensity that threatens to consume me.

The sound of activity draws me towards the kitchen, my heartbeat picking up speed as anticipation rattles through me. I long to see Sam, to hold her in my arms and kiss her senseless.

I enter the room silently, my breath catching in my throat at the sight that greets me. Sam stands behind the kitchen aisle, a piping bag in her hand as she carefully ices the top of a delicious-looking vanilla cake. Her phone sits nearby, a video of a famous pastry chef instructing her on the finer points of cake decoration.

My heart melts, a rush of emotion so powerful that it takes everything in me not to sweep her into my arms right then and there. Instead, I linger in the doorway, watching her work with unbridled enthusiasm, a side of her that few people get to see. This fierce, ruthless woman, who once threatened to stab a man with a broken bottle, is also sweet and loyal, a beguiling contradiction that captivates me completely.

"Looks delicious," I say playfully, a smile tugging at my lips.

Sam's gaze snaps to mine, startled by my sudden appearance. But then her face lights up, her lips stretching into a delighted grin. "It's keto-friendly, too." She snickers. "Happy birthday," she says with a shrug, a subtle pink hue tinging her cheeks.

I cross the room in a few long strides, slipping my arm around her waist the moment I'm close enough. Her body yields against mine, soft and pliant, the pastry sleeve falling forgotten onto the counter. "I... I'm not done yet... with the..." she mumbles, her eyes darkening with lust as they meet mine.

Unable to resist, I swipe my finger through the icing, gathering a dollop of sweetness before bringing it to her lips. Her mouth parts, allowing me to slip my finger inside, and I watch with rapt attention as she tastes the frosting. Then, before she can react, I lean in and capture her mouth with mine, my tongue teasing her lips apart and lapping at hers with tender strokes. The flavor of vanilla mingles with the unique taste of her, intoxicating me, stoking the embers of desire that always seem to smolder between us.

Slowly, reluctantly, I pull back, a smile playing at the corners of my mouth. "As I said," I purr, my voice low and rough, "delicious."

Sam takes a shaky breath, her eyes wide and dazed. "Whoa..." she whispers, pressing a hand to her chest. "That was nice."

I scowl, feigning offense. "Nice?"

"*More* than nice," she concedes, smoothing her hand along my arm, her touch soothing and electric all at once. "How are you feeling?"

"I'm good," I lie, not wanting to burden her with my worries, my fears about what's coming.

She licks her lips, a gesture that sends a bolt of heat straight to my core, before taking my hand and leading me to the breakfast room. We sit by the window, the sunlight casting a warm glow over her features, making her look even more ethereal than usual.

"So... I have a plan," she says, her voice brimming with confidence.

Surprise flickers through me, followed by a rush of affection. "A plan?" I echo, shaking my head. "Sam, really. I don't think we can prepare for any of this. Not when we don't have a clue what'll happen. No one alive has ever witnessed a Draken shift into his beast."

"And *that's* where you're wrong," she counters, leaning closer, her eyes alight with a knowing gleam. "There *is* someone who's witnessed a dragon shift. And not only that," she pauses for effect, her lips curving into a secretive smile, "she *married* him."

My eyes widen, awe and disbelief clashing within me. How did I not think of it sooner? "Juliette Deveraux," I mumble, meeting Sam's gaze head-on. "You spoke with the Grand Witch who just came back from the grave?" The thought makes me dizzy, but then again, it could just be my dragon awakening.

"I did," Sam confirms, her tone dry and matter-of-fact. "But don't worry. I told her nothing. I simply said I was curious as a witch to learn these things. And she was more than helpful." Pride and satisfaction radiate from her, a grin splitting her face. "And now, I have a plan."

"Okay," I breathe, my throat going dry as the reality of my impending shift hits me once more. "Just tell me what to do and I'll do it."

Sam flinches, her eyebrows shooting up in surprise. "Really? You'll do as I say?" A mischievous glint enters her eyes, her lips twitching with barely suppressed amusement. "In that case, my first order for you is that we have some cake. After I sing to you Happy Birthday."

I can't help but smile, her playful demeanor chasing away the shadows of my fear, if only for a moment. "You're gonna sing to me?"

"Mm-hmm," Sam nods, her nose crinkling adorably. "And you'll have to pretend to like it, as I'm a terrible singer."

I reach out and take her hand in mine, bringing it to my lips and pressing a tender kiss to her knuckles. "I don't think you could be terrible at anything, even if you tried."

A blush stains Sam's cheeks, a rosy hue that makes my heart skip a beat.

"I'm so happy you're here…" I tell her, my voice rough with emotion. *In my life,* I add silently, the words too big, too profound to voice aloud.

"I have a gift for you," she whispers, her tone low and intimate, sending a shiver down my spine.

"A gift?" I start, surprise and wonder filling me. "Sam, you've already spoiled me enough."

"It's never enough," she insists, her voice stern and unyielding. "Anyway, you've earned it."

Laughter bubbles up in my throat, clear and joyous. "Earned it?" I ask, my eyebrows shooting up in astonishment.

"Yeah," she confesses, utterly shameless. "I wouldn't be spoiling you had you turned out to be a jerk." She grins, throwing me a mischievous look that tells me she's not lying.

"Oh, I've *seen* how you treat jerks," I taunt, memories of that fateful night at the club flashing through my mind. "I'm just glad there are no bottles nearby."

She punches my arm, her lips pursing in a pout that I find utterly adorable. "That guy had it coming!"

"Ow!" I laugh, rubbing my arm in mock pain. "I know! I was there, remember?"

"Anyway," she continues, her eyes sparkling with excitement, "your gift."

"Yeah?" Curiosity burns through me, my heart racing in anticipation.

She slips her hand under the table, pulling out a classic red square jewelry box with gold detailing. *Cartier.*

"Sam," I breathe, stunned by the sight, by the implication of such an extravagant gift.

She tilts her head, delight dancing in her eyes as she takes in my astonishment. "Don't worry. I'm not proposing," she teases, grinning devilishly.

I crack a smile, even as my heart clenches with a bittersweet longing. *If only she were...*

"Open it," she urges, her voice soft and expectant.

With trembling fingers, I take the box and flip it open, my breath catching in my throat at the sight that greets me. There, nestled in the velvet lining, is a signet ring, the embodiment of my family's ancient legacy. The gold ring bears a meticulously chiseled dragon in a rampant pose, its wings spread wide and its mouth open in a silent roar. Flames curl around the beast, while tiny ruby eyes gleam with lifelike intensity. Intricate Celtic knotwork surrounds the dragon, and at the base, a motto is inscribed: "In Flammis Gloriam." *In flames, glory.*

"Wow," I mumble, overwhelmed by the thoughtfulness, the significance of such a gift.

Sam gives me a half-smile, her eyes shining with emotion. "I thought it would be fitting," she says softly. "I never imagined it would be *so* fitting." She slides closer, her hand coming up to cup the side of my face, her touch gentle and reverent. "You're the first dragon shifter in three hundred years, Nik. You might be the last dragon the world ever sees."

Her words hit me like a punch to the gut, tears burning at the back of my eyes. I swallow hard, trying to master the storm of emotions swirling inside me.

With infinite tenderness, Sam slips the ring onto my finger, the metal cool and heavy against my skin. "Never forget who you are," she whispers, her voice fierce with conviction. "Happy birthday, babe."

I tighten my grip on her hand, my anchor in a sea of uncertainty. "I don't know if I'll be the last dragon the world ever sees," I tell her, my voice raw and trembling. "But I know I'm the luckiest man in the world... because I have you."

And then I'm kissing her, slowly, tenderly, pouring all the love and gratitude and wonder I feel into the press of my lips against hers. Her peace washes over me, filling me up, chasing away the fears and doubts that plague me.

With Sam by my side, I feel like I can face anything. Even the terrifying unknown of my first shift.

Because together, we are unstoppable. Unbreakable.

And that is the greatest gift of all.

21

NIK

Night settles over us like a velvet cloak, the darkness broken only by the silvery glow of the moon and the myriad stars that dot the sky. We sit on the terrace overlooking the ocean, huddled together on the garden couch, a heavy wool blanket wrapped around our entwined bodies. The firepit crackles and pops, casting a warm, flickering light over our faces.

We've been silent for a while, the weight of anticipation hanging heavy in the air. Waiting for the unexpected, the inevitable. Not knowing how or when or even if *it* will happen.

The headache has returned, stronger than ever, but it's become such a constant companion that I barely register the pain anymore. It's just another reminder of the chaos that churns within me, the beast that threatens to break free at any moment.

Sam slips a warm mug between my hands, the heat seeping into my skin, grounding me in the present. But the silence grows tight with tension, and I can't stop the words that spill from my lips. "Are you sure about this? Would you not rather leave?"

She gives me a look, her eyes soft but unyielding. "Drink your tea," she says, dismissing the choice I offer, the out that I so desperately want her to take.

I bring the mug to my lips, inhaling the floral aroma that wafts up from the steaming liquid. Lavender and chamomile, with a hint of sweetness that makes my eyebrows lift in surprise. "Honey?" I ask, a faint frown now creasing my brow.

Sam bats her lashes, the picture of innocence. "Yes, dear?"

A snicker escapes me, warmth flooding my cheeks. Gods, she's merciless, taking such delight in making me blush.

"Yeah. I added honey," she admits, a smile playing at the corners of her mouth. "Juliette said it would sweeten your beast's temper."

I nod, taking another sip of the tea, letting the warmth spread through my body. "Is this going to make me drowsy right away?"

"No." She curls up against my chest, her head resting over my heart. "It's going to take a while for it to kick in. Juliette said she'd make sure Willem was out of the house whenever he looked like he was about to shift. But apparently, the guy was a shifter *pro*. He mastered his dragon at all times."

"I'll get there too, Sam," I assure her, my voice low and fervent. "I promise."

"I know you will." The conviction in her voice, the unwavering faith that shines in her eyes... it takes my breath away. I wish I had the same certainty, the same unshakable belief in myself.

I finish the tea and set the mug aside, my arms coming up to wrap around her, holding her close. "Alright," I whisper, leaning in until our faces are just inches apart, our breath mingling in the cool night air. "I'm ready for... whatever."

"It's Juliette's recipe, so it has to work... right?" Sam mumbles, her brow furrowing with a hint of uncertainty. "Gods, I hope she remembered correctly. I mean, the woman has been dead for three hundred years..."

A faint sense of alarm shoots through me at the hesitation in her voice, the flicker of doubt that crosses her face. "Sam?"

She starts, shaking her head as if to clear it. "No, no... Everything's gonna be all right, babe. I promise."

"*Babe* again?" I tease, trying to lighten the mood, to chase away the shadows that linger in her eyes. "That's what you're calling me?"

She purses her lips, a hint of concern creasing her brow. "You don't like it?"

I shoot up an eyebrow, a smirk tugging at my mouth. "I mean, it's hot..."

"*You're* hot," she interrupts, her eyes sparkling with mischief.

The blush returns with a vengeance, heat flooding my face. "Okay, now you're just having fun."

"A little..." She giggles, nuzzling her face against my chest, her warmth seeping into my skin through the thin fabric of my shirt.

I tighten my arm around her, pressing her closer, my lips brushing the shell of her ear. "You're a feisty little bear," I purr, my voice low and rough. "*My* feisty Little Bear."

"Your Little Bear," she echoes, her voice soft and sweet. "I like that."

"It's fitting, isn't it?" I muse, a smile tugging at my lips. "You, the fierce and frosty bear from the Russian clan, and me, the fiery dragon shifter."

Sam laughs, the sound like music to my ears. "Fire and ice," she says, turning in my arms to face me, her eyes sparkling with mirth and affection. "We're quite the pair, aren't we?"

"We are," I agree, my hand coming up to cup her cheek, my thumb stroking the soft, smooth skin. "But you know what they say about opposites attracting."

"And what's that?" she asks, her lips curving into a playful smirk.

"That when fire and ice come together, they create

something beautiful, something powerful," I murmur, my voice low and intense. "Something that can't be broken or destroyed."

Sam's breath hitches, her eyes widening as she takes in my words. "You really believe that?" she whispers, her voice trembling slightly.

"I do," I say, my gaze locked on hers, unwavering and sure. "I believe in us, Sam. In the strength of what we have."

She smiles then, a radiant, heart-stopping smile that makes my pulse race and my heart soar. "I believe in us too," she says softly, her hand coming up to cover mine where it rests on her cheek. "Fire and ice, dragon and bear... you and me."

Gods, her nearness is driving me wild, desire coiling hot and heavy in my gut. Images of last night flash through my mind, memories of our bodies tangled together, lost in the throes of passion. "So, um... what are we gonna do now?" I manage, my voice strained with the effort of holding back. "Just sit around the firepit and wait?"

Sam bites her lower lip, her eyes darkening with hunger. Her hands come up to cup my face, her thumbs stroking over my cheekbones as she leans in, her lips brushing against mine in a soft, tender kiss.

And just like that, all my worries fade away, the tension melting from my body as I lose myself in the sweetness of her kiss. Nothing else matters but this moment, this connection, the love that burns between us like an unquenchable flame.

Slowly, the hunger grows, my kiss turning deeper, more demanding. I sweep her into my arms, lifting her effortlessly, a low growl rumbling in my chest as she straddles my waist, her thighs clenching around me.

"Oh, gods. Sam..." I groan against her mouth, my hands roaming over her curves, mapping the contours of her sensual body.

"Uh-huh," she breathes, molding herself against me, her fingers slipping beneath my shirt, tracing the planes of my chest.

"I want you," I manage, my voice rough with need, with the desperation that claws at my insides.

"Me too..." She tugs at my shirt, yanking it over my head and tossing it aside. In a flash, I'm on my feet, the blanket falling to the grass as I lift her with me, ready to lay her down and worship every inch of her body.

I ease her onto the blanket, my eyes drinking in the sight of her, chest heaving, lips parted, eyes dark with desire. My hands glide up her thighs, pushing her skirt out of the way.

"Yes," she moans, arching up into my touch. "Gods, yes..."

I reach for my belt, my fingers fumbling with the buckle, my entire body thrumming with need. But then, out of the corner of my eye, I catch a flicker of movement, a spark of light that makes me pause.

At first, I think it's just the firepit—embers drifting on the night breeze. But as I turn my hands over, my heart stops, my breath catching in my throat.

Cinders peel off my palms, glowing bright and hot as they float up into the air around us. And then, before I can even begin to process what's happening, a wave of heat crashes over me, so intense that it steals the air from my lungs.

My arms and chest start to gleam, the same bright red as the night before, but this time, the light only grows brighter, the heat more intense with each passing second. It's like there's a fire burning inside me, consuming me from the inside out, and I can't breathe, can't think, can't do anything but gasp for air that won't come.

Sam sits up, her eyes wide with fear, her face awash in shades of ivory and pink as the glow from my skin casts an eerie light over her features. Her maroon eyes are the last thing I see before the world fades away, swallowed up by the darkness that descends like a crushing weight.

And then, there is nothing. No sound, no light, no sensation. Just an endless, yawning void that stretches out before me, beckoning me into its depths.

I try to fight it, try to claw my way back to consciousness, back to Sam. But it's like swimming through molasses, like trying to run in a dream. No matter how hard I struggle, I can't seem to break free, can't seem to find my way back to the surface.

Panic claws at my throat, a scream building in my chest, but it's trapped, locked inside me, unable to escape. And still, the darkness presses in, thick and heavy and suffocating.

I'm drowning, sinking deeper and deeper into the abyss, and there's nothing I can do to stop it. Nothing I can do to save myself.

Just when I think all hope is lost, just when I'm sure that I'll be lost forever in this endless sea of black... *I feel it.* A spark, deep within me. A flicker of light in the darkness, small at first, but growing brighter with each passing second. It's warm and familiar, like coming home after a long journey. Like the first rays of sunlight after a stormy night.

And as it grows, as it spreads through my body like wildfire, I realize what it is—my dragon. My beast. The part of me that I've been running from, the part that I've been so afraid to embrace.

But now, as it rises up inside me, as it fills me with a strength and power that I've never known... I'm not afraid anymore.

I am the beast. The beast is me.

22

SAM

A *dragon.* A full-size firebreather rises before me, its form shimmering with an otherworldly glow, scales gleaming like burnished gold in the moonlight. For an instant, I'm awestruck, my mind reeling as it tries to process the impossible sight before me. But then, as the reality of the situation sinks in, panic slams into me like a tidal wave, icy fingers of fear clawing at my throat.

"Oh, fuck..." I murmur, my voice barely above a whisper as I take a slow, cautious step back from the mythical creature standing just a few feet away.

The dragon's wings rustle, the sound like the whisper of a thousand silk banners in the wind. It backs away, guided by some primal instinct, until it reaches the center of the vast front lawn. And there, it straightens to its full height, its powerful neck arching, its chest puffed out in a display of dominance and strength. With a sudden, violent gust of wind, its scintillating wings unfurl, stretching out to their full span, and the force of it nearly knocks me off my feet.

The warm air whips through my hair, tossing it around my face in wild tangles, but I barely notice. All I can do is stare, my eyes fixed on the mighty beast before me, a creature that no mortal has laid eyes on in centuries.

What the hell do I do now? My mind races, panic and confusion warring within me. I know my way around bear shifters, but dragons? This is so far beyond my realm of experience that I can barely even begin to wrap my head around it. I swallow hard, my throat dry and tight, as I take in the sheer size of the firebreather—its colossal form looming over the surrounding trees, its head nearly reaching the top of the manor's towering roof.

The dragon sways its head, looking almost as bewildered as I feel. Its slanted pupils narrow, glinting in the moonlight as it examines its own body, taking in the powerful limbs, the long, sinuous tail that coils behind it, the scales that gleam like polished gold.

It's breathtaking. Terrifying, yes, but also so heart-stoppingly beautiful that it steals the air from my lungs.

"Oh, boy..." I breathe, the words slipping out before

I can stop them. This is more shocking than that first dino scene in Jurassic Park, more surreal than anything I could have ever imagined.

The creature's neck swings towards me, its head cocking to the side as it locks eyes with me. Intelligence gleams in those dark, fathomless depths, a spark of something that's not quite human, but not entirely animal either.

"Okay... So, you heard that." I lick my lips, trying to keep my expression neutral, my voice steady. "That's some fine hearing."

A low growl rumbles in the creature's chest, the sound vibrating through the air, through my bones. It studies me, its gaze intense and unwavering, and I can't help but wonder if it's trying to decide whether I'm prey or predator.

"Nik," I breathe, my body frozen in place, my heart hammering against my ribs. "Nik, do you know who I am?" The words feel foolish, inadequate, but I have to try. Have to reach him somehow, even if it seems impossible.

The growl deepens, growing into a roar that shakes the very ground beneath my feet. And then, with a slow, deliberate motion, the dragon unhinges its jaw, revealing rows upon rows of razor-sharp teeth. Just like in the movies, the creature's throat begins to glow, the light shifting from a deep, smoldering red to a brilliant, blinding yellow as the fire within its belly rises up, spilling into its maw.

Instinct takes over, and I dash behind the stone bench, throwing myself to the ground just as a stream of white-hot flame erupts from the dragon's mouth. The heat of it sears my skin, singeing my hair, and I can smell the acrid stench of melting stone as the balustrade crumbles under the onslaught.

My breath comes in sharp, ragged gasps, panic clawing at my insides. "I don't think that's Nik anymore." This isn't the man I know and love. This is a beast, a creature of myth and legend.

"Fuck!" I hiss, my hands shaking as I try to pull myself together, to think past the fear that clouds my mind. It's all I can do not to give in to the terror that threatens to consume me.

The tea. Juliette's recipe. It has to do *something*, right? But how long will it take to kick in? How long before the dragon's temper is soothed, before the man I love comes back to me?

"Nik!" I peer over the bench, my heart in my throat.

The dragon cocks its massive head, its eyes narrowing. Does it recognize the name? Does some part of it remember who it used to be? I can't tell, and the uncertainty is maddening.

But I'm desperate, willing to try anything to calm the beast that wears my lover's heart. Juliette's words echo in my mind, a mantra that I cling to like a lifeline. "Willem mastered his beast—*but I tamed the dragon.*"

I suck in a deep breath, summoning every ounce of courage I possess. "I *will* tame you, firebreather," I say, my teeth clenched in determination.

Rising to my feet, I square my shoulders, my chin lifted in defiance. "Nik!" I shout, the little bear inside me growling in challenge. "You're being a bad dragon right now!"

The beast leans forward, keeping a safe distance, and for a moment, I wonder if it's as wary of me as I am of it. Good. Let it be afraid. Let it know that I'm not some helpless damsel waiting to be rescued.

But then, its nostrils flare, and a gust of hot, stinging air slams into me, flinging me back like a rag doll. I hit the stone balustrade hard, the impact driving the breath from my lungs, and for a moment, all I can do is cling to the rough-hewn stone, my fingers scrabbling for purchase.

One glance over my shoulder, and my blood runs cold. The drop behind me is dizzying, the jagged rocks below promising a quick and painful death. If I had fallen...

Anger surges through me, hot and fierce, chasing away the last lingering tendrils of fear. My jaw clenches, my muscles coiling tight as I push myself upright, my hands balled into fists at my sides.

I'm a formidable witch, or so I've been told, my

power growing stronger with each passing day. But in this moment, facing down a creature of legend, I feel woefully unprepared. My mind races, searching for any scrap of knowledge, any whisper of a spell or incantation that might help me tame the beast before me.

But there's nothing. No ancient wisdom passed down through generations, no secret rituals hidden away in dusty tomes. Juliette, for all her talk of taming dragons, never mentioned if there were any magical means to do so.

I'm flying blind, armed with nothing but my wits and my stubborn refusal to give up. It's a daunting prospect, but I can't let it shake me. I won't let it break me.

I yank down my skirt, smoothing the fabric with a sharp, irritated motion, and then I'm marching forward, my steps fueled by a newfound determination. If Juliette could tame her dragon, then damn it, so can I. I won't let this beast, this creature of smoke and flame, take Nik away from me. Not now, not ever.

The firebreather snorts, a plume of smoke curling from its nostrils. And then, slowly, inexorably, its mouth begins to open, the fiery glow building in the back of its throat once more.

Here we go again.

Fuck. It's going to be a long night.

But I won't back down. I won't give up. Not on Nik, not on us.

I am Samara Alexeev, daughter of great bears and talented witches. I have faced worse than this, and I have survived.

And I will survive this too, no matter what it takes.

So bring it on, dragon. Give me your worst.

I'm ready for you.

23
DRAGON

Burn...
Destroy...
Play?

24

SAM

My skin prickles in the morning light, the tingling sensation sharpening until it becomes a searing pain, like a thousand needles stabbing into my arm. The agony forces my eyes open, and as consciousness returns, so do the memories of the night before: the violent blaze of fire and smoke, roaring flames licking at the elm trees, Nik's dragon chasing me across the lawn...

I find myself lying on a heap of straw in the stables, my body aching and sore. Slowly, I sit up, wincing as the movement strains my arm and shoulder. "Ow!" I cry out, looking down at my forearm. The skin is tender and gleaming bright red, a painful reminder of the ordeal I've endured.

"Oh, gods..." I groan, struggling to my feet, the burn stinging like hell. "Nik, you better keep some aloe in the kitchen," I grumble, combing my fingers through my tangled hair as I trudge out of the stables.

It wasn't Nik's fault, my injury. His dragon had thought it would be *great fun* to light up the greenhouse, and I just happened to be in the wrong place at the wrong time, running away from the rampaging beast like a kitten chased by an over-enthusiastic toddler. My arm had brushed against the scorching metal door, and the pain had been excruciating. It still is.

I climb the front steps to the porch, noting with a dull sense of surprise that the door is open. I'm too exhausted, too drained, both physically and emotionally, to puzzle out what that might mean. So I simply walk inside, my steps heavy and dragging.

As I enter the vestibule, the sound of heavy footsteps echoes from above, a frantic staccato that sets my nerves on edge. I hear doors slamming, the thud of feet pounding down the hallway, a muffled curse that carries through the stillness. Nik is searching for me, his movements erratic and desperate, and I can almost feel the panic radiating from him, the fear that grips his heart.

The footsteps grow louder, closer, until they're thundering down the stairs, each step a hammer blow against the polished wood. And then he's there, frozen at the top of the staircase, his chest heaving, his eyes wide and wild as they scan the room below.

For a moment, he doesn't see me, his gaze skipping

over my still form as if I'm nothing more than a shadow, a trick of the light. I stand perfectly motionless, watching him with weary eyes, taking in the disheveled state of his hair, the wrinkled fabric of his shirt, the dark circles that mar the perfection of his face.

But then, as if sensing my presence, his head snaps towards me, his eyes locking onto mine with an intensity that steals my breath. Relief and joy and terror and a thousand other emotions flicker across his face in rapid succession, each one a mirror of the chaos that reigns in my own heart.

"Sam!" Nik rushes down the stairs to meet me, his voice thick with relief and concern. "Sam, I was so worried! I've been looking for you all morning!"

I brace myself for the impact of his embrace, for the warmth of his arms around me and the desperate press of his lips against mine. But as he draws closer, I become acutely aware of my own disheveled state, a flush of shame heating my cheeks.

Despite the chaos of the night before, despite his disheveled state, and the fear and exhaustion that must surely be weighing on him, Nik looks as handsome and radiant as ever. But me? I'm a hot mess, my clothes filthy and torn, my skin smudged with dirt and ash. My burnt arm throbs with every beat of my heart.

And my hair... gods, my hair. It hangs in limp, tangled strands around my face, reeking of smoke and sweat. I can't help but wrinkle my nose in disgust. I desperately need a long, hot bath.

When he reaches me, his ice-blue eyes scan my body from head to toe, taking in every scrape and bruise. And then, inevitably, he notices my sore arm. Nik's expression slackens, his eyes widening in horror as he gasps in outright dismay. "You're injured..." he mumbles, shock giving way to a deep, aching pain that etches itself across his handsome features.

"It's nothing..." I try to dismiss his concern, not wanting to add to the guilt I can already see weighing on his shoulders.

"Don't say that!" he growls, his voice rough with emotion. Nik's hand flies to his mouth, his face flushing as his eyes fill with tears, one spilling down his cheek, a wordless expression of the depths of his agony.

He tilts his head to the side, the gesture so reminiscent of his dragon form that it makes my heart clench. Nik leans closer, cupping the side of my face with his hand, his touch infinitely gentle despite the turmoil I can see raging in his eyes. "Sam," he whispers, my name falling from his lips like a prayer and a plea all at once. "If I can't control this beast... If I can't... then... maybe we shouldn't..."

I see where this conversation is headed, and a deep, visceral dread settles in the pit of my stomach. A frown creases my brow, my heart seizing in my chest. "Shut up," I cut him off, shaking my head vehemently. "Don't you dare say those words." My throat clenches tight, making it hard to breathe, to think past the panic rising like bile in my throat.

"Sam, I hurt you…" he whispers, wariness deepening his pitch, his eyes shadowed with a pain that mirrors my own. "And I can't even remember it!"

"You *will* be able to control it," I assure him, smoothing a hand along his muscular arm, trying to anchor him with my touch, my certainty. "I know you will. It just… takes time."

"Time?" He scowls, frustration and fear warring in his eyes. "I don't even know when I will shift again… My dragon could kill you!" A glazed look of despair spreads across his face, and it breaks my heart to see him so lost, so afraid.

"Yeah, tell me about it." I shrug, trying to lighten the mood, to chase away the shadows that cling to him. "It almost threw me off the terrace."

"What?" He flinches, concern twisting his features, his hands tightening on my shoulders.

I squeeze my eyes shut and let out a deep, exasperated sigh. Why did I have to bring that up? I mentally berate myself for being so reckless. "Listen, if it's anything like the Ursa shifting, it won't happen anytime soon…" I try to reassure him, though I can tell my words are falling on deaf ears. "It can take months for the second shift to happen."

Nik takes my hands in his, pressing them against his

lips in a gesture that's both tender and desperate. He lowers them slowly, his ocean eyes locked on mine, a world of emotion swirling in their depths. "I won't put you through this, Little Bear..." he breathes, his voice breaking on the endearment. Nik purses his lips, an adorable dimple piercing his left cheek, but the resolute set of his jaw belies the pain I know he's feeling. "I just won't."

I feel like I've been sucker-punched, the air rushing out of my lungs in a whoosh. "What are you saying?" I manage, my heart shattering into a million jagged pieces.

"I'm saying," he whispers, each word like a dagger to my soul, "you're better off without me. *That's* what I'm saying."

Shock reverberates through me, followed swiftly by a wave of nauseating dread. "You're... You're breaking up with me?"

He remains silent, his eyes saying everything his lips cannot.

Pain and worry strain me through and through, my vision blurring with unshed tears. "Nik...?" I breathe.

As my world crumbles around me, something steals my attention—a flicker of movement in the corner of my eye. A familiar SUV pulls into the driveway, and my blood turns to ice in my veins as I recognize the figure behind the wheel: the fiercest Ursa fighter the Elite team has ever known.

Dima.

"Oh, fuck..." I mumble, my heart seizing with a new kind of terror.

"Listen, it's not easy on me either..." Nik adds, but his words are drowned out by the roaring in my ears.

My mouth goes slack, my mind reeling as I try to process this new development. How would they know where to find me? "How...?" I manage, my voice barely above a whisper.

"Huh?" Nik frowns, confusion creasing his brow.

"Nik..." I begin, ready to explain, to beg for his understanding, when the manor's front doors burst open with a resounding bang. I wince, knowing exactly what's coming... or rather, who.

My brother's heavy footsteps echo in the double-height vestibule as he storms in, his face a thundercloud of rage. Sheer black dread splinters through my bones, turning my knees to jelly.

Even then, I muster the courage to step in front of Nik, shielding him with my body, my hands raised in a placating gesture. "Gavriil, let me explain..." I say, hoping against hope to appease his fury.

But then, to my astonishment, Nik's hand smooths over my shoulder, gently easing me aside as he steps forward to face my brother, his chin lifted in sheer defiance.

"Get your filthy talons off my sister!" Gavriil roars, his face flushed with outrage. I pray to all the gods that he doesn't do something rash, something we'll all regret.

Nik's impassive eyes fix on the Ursa King, tracking his movements as he grabs my arm and yanks me towards him, his harsh grip bruising in its intensity.

Gavriil ignores my disarray and pulls me behind him, lunging forward until he's nose-to-nose with Nik, his teeth bared in a snarl. "Do not think for one second I will let this pass," he hisses, his voice dripping with venom. "Bram will be hearing from me soon!"

"Please!" I beg, my heart shattering into a million pieces, the pain worse than any physical wound could ever be. "Gavriil! *Please*, listen to me!"

My brother's head snaps towards me, his fierce eyes blazing with fury. "Do not speak another word," he tells me in our mother tongue, his tone smooth but no less harsh for its beauty. By choosing to speak in Russian, he's deliberately shutting Nik out, creating a wall between us that feels insurmountable.

Gavriil's wrath consumes him entirely, rendering him oblivious to my sore arm, and for that small mercy, I am grateful. I shudder to think of the mounting rage he would unleash if he knew the extent of my burns.

"Let's go!" he barks at me, still in Russian, his fingers digging into my skin with bruising force. I flinch, knowing that any resistance will only make him angrier.

"Please, don't..." I insist in the lowest of voices,

knowing full well it will be useless. Once my brother has made up his mind, there's no changing it, no swaying him from his course.

Nik's brooding eyes follow me as my brother drags me towards the door, ocean blue and glistening with undiluted pain. He opens his mouth as if to speak, but hesitates—torn between his desperate need to stop Gavriil and his desire to protect me from himself. Nik knows I am safest far away from him. It's an excruciating battle, and I am caught in the crossfire.

The realization that he's willing to let me go, to sacrifice our love for my safety, is like a knife to the heart. As soon as it sinks in, I stop fighting, the strength draining out of me like water through a sieve. Warm tears trickle down my face, blurring my vision as I turn towards the door, each step like a dagger in my soul.

I'm leaving behind my greatest love, the man who holds my heart in his hands. I'm saying goodbye to the purest happiness I've ever known, the joy and peace I found in Nik's arms.

And as the door closes behind me, shutting me off from the warmth of his presence, I feel a part of myself wither and die, turning to ash in the face of this unbearable loss.

But even through the pain, through the soul-deep ache that threatens to consume me, one truth remains, bright and shining and unshakable.

I love him. I will always love him.

25

SAM

Tears stream down my face as I sit in silence inside the car, my heart shattered into a million jagged pieces. I wouldn't dream of letting my brother see me cry, but I can't seem to stop the flow of emotions that pour out of me, as unstoppable as a river in flood. Gavriil slides into the Rolls-Royce Phantom SUV. He sits beside me, his face stoic and unreadable, seemingly untouched by the situation now that his rampage against Nik has ended.

The sound of Dima closing the door barely registers through the haze of my grief, and I hear the crunch of gravel under his feet as he moves around the vehicle, the driver's door opening and closing as he settles behind the wheel.

Through the blur of my tears, I catch a glimpse of Dima's dark green eyes in the rearview mirror, shining with worry and concern as he watches me. But I can't bear the weight of his gaze, can't stand the pity I see there. So I turn away, staring out the tinted window at the world beyond, a world that feels cold and empty without Nik by my side.

As the car's engine rumbles to life, I take a small measure of comfort in the knowledge that it's just Gavriil, Dima, and Sasha following in his black BMW. My brother's security detail is minimal, but then again, he hardly needs more than a fierce Enforcer and the head of the clan's Elite. The rest is just for show, a display of power and strength that's as much about intimidation as it is about protection.

And besides, I know Gavriil wouldn't want word to get out about my relationship with Nik. The Ursa clan would be in an uproar if they knew I was sleeping with the enemy, and my brother's position as leader would be called into question.

When the privacy screen rolls up with a soft whir, I heave a sigh, my shoulders slumping under the weight of my exhaustion and heartbreak. As if facing a frisky dragon wasn't enough, now I have to deal with a rabid bear, my brother's anger and disapproval like a physical presence in the car.

I shut my eyes, childishly hoping that by closing them, I can make Gavriil disappear, just like I used to do when we were kids and we'd get into a fight.

But of course, it didn't work then, and it doesn't work now.

"He's a Draken, Samara!" Gavriil mutters, his voice tight with barely contained rage. "A Draken!"

I glare at him, too exhausted and hurt to speak, to defend myself or my choices. It's not as if my brother expects me to say anything anyway. He's the mighty Ursa King—he *will* be heard.

He combs his fingers through his long chestnut hair, a gesture of frustration and agitation, before leaning towards me, his face inches from mine. "Do you understand we're at war with this family?" he says through clenched teeth, his voice low and deadly. "Why? Why would you tarnish our name with this... unspeakable betrayal?"

"Gavriil..." I manage, my voice barely above a whisper, but he cuts me off with a sharp gesture.

"No!" he explodes, his eyes flashing with fierce fury. "I don't want to hear any excuses! Whatever you had with that monster is officially over."

He straightens, returning to his seat, but his words linger in the air between us, a pronouncement of doom that makes my blood run cold.

"He's not a monster..." I mutter, my voice small and broken, but filled with a quiet defiance.

Gavriil starts, his eyes widening in disbelief. "Excuse me?"

"No more than you and I are monsters," I add, my

tone gloomy and resigned. I know better than to meet his gaze, to challenge him openly.

"Samara!" he snaps, his voice cracking like a whip, silencing me. I jump, my heart racing in my chest. "You will never see him again. Is that understood?"

He searches my face, looking for some sign of acquiescence, but I refuse to meet his eyes, knowing that it will only fuel his anger. He's the alpha, the leader of our clan, and his word is law.

I nod in silence, fresh tears spilling down my cheeks as I blink, too tired and heartbroken to explain that there's nothing left between Nik and me anyway. He broke up with me, pushed me away... and the pain of it is almost more than I can bear.

"Say it," Gavriil insists, his voice cold and unyielding. He's become so cruel since Luciana's death, so hard and unforgiving.

"Understood," I say through gritted teeth, a low growl rumbling in my throat. I'm so furious, so hurt and angry, that I'm growling like a bear... and suddenly, the memory of Nik calling me his Little Bear floods my mind, bringing with it a fresh wave of grief.

Oh, gods... what has he done? What have *we* done?

I lose my composure completely, sobbing into my hands. Then I hug my arms around myself, as if I can somehow hold the broken pieces of my heart together through sheer force of will.

Gavriil nods, satisfied. "Good."

As the SUV drives down the long entrance to the property, the evidence of last night's chaos is everywhere. Burnt trees and carbonized stone arches line the way, boulders and rubble piled up near the road. It looks like a war zone, like something out of a post-apocalyptic nightmare.

"Look at the state of this place," my brother sneers, his lip curling in derision as he surveys the destruction. "The Drakens truly must be ruined if they can't even afford good landscaping."

I remain silent, too lost in my own misery to respond.

"I bet it's that warlock's fault, Bram," Gavriil continues, his voice dripping with contempt. "He's been splurging through the family's fortune ever since he took over their clan. Some lousy leader he turned out to be, wasting his money on booze and women."

Still, I say nothing, my gaze fixed on the world outside the window, a world that feels as bleak and empty as my own shattered heart.

"You're better off away from them," Gavriil adds, his tone softening just a fraction, as if he's trying to comfort me in his own twisted way.

I bite my lower lip, fighting back a fresh wave of tears. Because the truth is, Nik feels exactly the same way. He thinks I'm better off without him, that I'm safer and happier far away from the chaos and danger of his world.

And maybe they're both right. Maybe I am better off alone, without the constant threat of dragons and bears and the weight of centuries of hatred and mistrust.

But as the car speeds away from the only place I've ever truly felt at home, from the man who holds my heart in his hands... I can't help but feel like I'm leaving a piece of myself behind, like I'm abandoning the one thing that makes me feel whole and alive.

And I don't know if I'll ever be the same again, don't know if I'll ever find my way back to the happiness and peace I found in Nik's arms.

But I do know one thing, with a certainty that burns bright and fierce in my chest.

I will never stop loving him.

26

SAM

I'm lying in my bedroom's bay window, my eyes fixed on the snowflakes that drift past, slowly painting the driveway a pristine white. The cold seeps through the glass, chilling my skin, but I barely feel it. I'm numb, inside and out, my heart frozen in the aftermath of losing Nik.

It's been days, maybe weeks, since I last left the beach house. I've lost track of time, the hours blurring together in a haze of misery and despair. What's the point of keeping count, when every moment is a reminder of what I've lost, of the love that's been ripped away from me?

The buzz of Yule preparations fills the household, the excitement all but tangible in the air. The Deveraux witches are hosting a dinner party, and we're invited—a summons that cannot be refused. But the thought of facing the world, of pretending to be happy and whole when I'm shattered inside... it's almost more than I can bear.

Gavriil, of course, has made it clear that I have no say in the matter. No surprise there. My brother has become a tyrant, a man who demands obedience and compliance at every turn.

But it's not the party that weighs on my mind, not the thought of facing the Deverauxs and their insufferable superiority. No, it's the silence from Nik that cuts me to the core, the lack of any word or sign that he's thinking of me, missing me the way I miss him.

Was it really that easy for him to move on, to forget what we had? How can he pretend that our love was anything less than extraordinary, a once-in-a-lifetime kind of connection?

Gods, I don't think he's having a hard time being apart. Not like I am, not like I'm drowning in the pain of his absence, suffocating under the weight of my own broken heart.

The creak of my bedroom door jolts me from my thoughts, and I hear a familiar voice call out, "Sam?"

I don't look back, don't want to see the pity in my friend's eyes. "Mila," I say, my tone dull and lifeless.

I've been keeping my distance from her ever since I got back from Brittany, ever since my world imploded in a fiery blaze of heartache and betrayal. She knows the reason, knows the role she played in tearing me away from Nik.

"Can I come in?" she asks, her voice tentative, unsure.

I want to tell her no, to scream at her to leave me alone with my misery. But I purse my lips instead, swallowing back the bitter words that rise in my throat.

"Sam..." she continues, and out of the corner of my eye, I see her ambling towards me, something green clutched in her hands. "I'm sorry about what happened..."

My head snaps towards her, and I fix her with a menacing glare, the anger that's been simmering inside me finally boiling over. "Was it you?" I demand, my voice sharp and accusing. "Just admit it."

I'm so certain she's the one to blame, the one who ratted me out to Gavriil. It could be no one else. Only she knew where I was staying. Only she had the power to betray my trust so completely.

"No, of course not!" Mila pleads, her blonde curls bouncing as she kneels by my side, her eyes wide and desperate. "How can you think that of me?"

"Well, for starters, your brother was there," I mumble, my tone aloof and distant. "I saw *him* first."

"Sam, please believe me! It wasn't me!" Mila grabs my arm, her fingers digging into my skin. "My sister, she was so worried that covering for you would get us into trouble with Gavriil. She must have called Dima..."

A frown furrows my brow, confusion warring with the anger that still simmers in my veins.

"I didn't know a thing about Gavriil coming over to find you," Mila continues, her words tumbling out in a rush. "I swear! Dima told me about it only after you returned to Paris!"

Her pink lips quiver, tears rimming her eyes, and I feel a flicker of doubt, a tiny spark of hope that maybe, just maybe, I've been wrong about her all along.

"Please, Sam," she begs, her voice breaking. "Tell me you believe me!"

My expression softens, the anger draining away as quickly as it came. I take Mila's hands in mine, the holiday wreath she was carrying falling forgotten to the floor.

"Oh Mila," I whisper, my throat tight with unshed tears. "It was awful... It's all a mess!"

I leap down from the window, falling into her arms, and she holds me tight, her embrace warm and comforting. And just like that, the floodgates open, and I'm weeping like I did when I left Nik, my body shaking with the force of my sobs.

"I love him, Mila," I choke out, biting my lip to hold back the wail that threatens to escape. "And I've lost him forever!"

Tears spill down my cheeks, hot and bitter, a physical manifestation of the grief that consumes me.

"I'm so sorry, sweetie," Mila murmurs, her voice soft

and soothing. She pulls back, locking eyes with me, a tiny smile playing at the corners of her mouth. "Hey. Maybe you'll run into him tonight?"

Her words spark a flicker of interest, a tiny ember of hope that refuses to be extinguished. "Tonight?" I ask, narrowing my eyes in confusion. What the devil is she talking about?

"At Deveraux Manor," she explains, as if it should be obvious. But I'm still in the dark, my mind too clouded by heartache to make the connection.

"Huh?" I wrinkle my nose, wondering if Mila has finally lost her mind.

"At the Yule party?" she prompts, giving me a knowing look.

And just like that, it clicks. My eyes widen, my stomach dropping like a stone. "That's tonight?" I gasp, my heart racing in my chest. *Oh, my fucking gods.*

"Yeah..." Mila shrugs, as if it's no big deal. But to me, it's everything.

A glimmer of hope blooms in my chest, a tiny flame that refuses to be extinguished. I try to tamp it down, to keep my expectations in check, but I can't fight the feeling that maybe, just maybe, this is the chance I've been waiting for.

The chance to see Nik again, to look into his eyes and make him understand how wrong he was to push me away, to shut me out of his life.

I love him, all of him, dragon and man alike. And I'll be damned if I let him go without a fight.

"Gods, Mila! You're wonderful!" I exclaim, leaping to my feet, a renewed sense of purpose coursing through my veins. "I'll see Nik tonight!"

I swipe at my tears with the back of my hand, smearing black mascara across my skin. But I don't care. Nothing matters but the possibility of being near him again, of feeling the warmth of his presence and the touch of his hand.

"Not looking like this, you're not," Mila teases, plucking the holly wreath from the floor and placing it on my head like a crown. "Come on. I'll help you get ready."

I sniff, feeling the heat of a blush rising in my cheeks. "You're right. I must look dreadful. I gotta look fabulous for my dragon..."

Mila starts, her brow furrowing in confusion. "Your... *dragon*?"

My mouth goes slack, panic flaring in my chest. "Uh... That's what I call him," I amend quickly, scrambling for an explanation. "He calls me his Little Bear."

A smile tugs at my lips, the memory of Nik's endearment warming me from the inside out.

"Aw! That's so sweet!" Mila coos, pressing a hand to her heart.

"Yeah." I give her a brief smile, relief washing over me. That was close. Too close.

If my clan knew the truth about Nik, about the beast that lies beneath his skin... they would go ballistic. And Gavriil... gods, I don't even want to think about how he would react. It would be a bloodbath, a war between our families that would tear the supernatural world apart.

But as Mila tugs me towards my closet, chattering excitedly about dresses and hairstyles, I push those thoughts aside.

Tonight, none of that matters. Tonight, all that exists is the hope burning in my chest, the love that refuses to be denied.

Tonight, I'll see my dragon again. And one way or another, I'll make him see the truth.

That we belong together, now and always.

No matter what the world throws our way.

27

SAM

When the knock on my door came, I opened it to find a stylist waiting in the hallway, a garment bag draped over her arm. It came as no surprise that Gavriil had already arranged everything concerning my attire for the evening, from the gown itself to the hair and makeup. My brother has always been the attentive type, some might say a tad controlling. As the Ursa King's sister, he would expect nothing less than perfection from me at the Deveraux's dinner party.

The thought makes me grin with a hint of rebellious pride as I walk through the manor's threshold, into the witches' lair. If only Gavriil knew the truth about the slob I really am.

The splendor of our home in Saint Petersburg pales in comparison to Deveraux Manor, and that's saying something. With its imposing marble halls, wide spaces, and exquisite decorations, this place rivals any palace I've ever seen.

It's the second time this house has gathered Alexeevs, Deverauxs, and Drakens under one roof. The seance went well enough, if by *well* you mean no bloodshed. But I can't shake the feeling of walking on eggshells. The sense that the peace between our families is more fragile than ever.

I pause at the terrace's threshold, marveling at the magical display before me. Amber string lights tangle in the trees, their glow casting a warm, inviting light over the scene. Votive candles line the staircase leading down to the lawn, where a high white tent stands in the middle of the courtyard, a dozen crystal chandeliers hanging from its ceiling.

The music is soft and lulling, drawing me in. I step closer to the balustrade, my eyes sweeping over the crowd of gorgeous warlocks and witches below. And there, skulking in the shadows, is a vampire. Dristan, I remember from the seance. He's a charming one, an outcast in our world. Maybe I should go say hi...

"Samara," a familiar voice calls out, interrupting my musings.

I turn, a smile blooming on my lips as I see my brother striding towards me. "Vlad!" I exclaim, surprised and delighted by his presence. "You're here, in Paris!"

Volodya opens his arms, and I take a moment to appreciate his impeccable tux, the white gold cufflinks, the bespoke shoes that probably cost more than most people make in a month. He looks like he just stepped out of the pages of GQ magazine.

I all but launch myself into Vlad's waiting arms, desperate for the comfort and familiarity of his embrace. As his strong arms wrap around me, enveloping me in a cocoon of safety and love, I feel some of the tension drain from my body, the knots of anxiety and loneliness that have taken up residence in my chest loosening just a fraction.

"Anya sends her regards," Vlad murmurs, his voice low and reassuring, and I can't help but smile at the mention of my sister-in-law. But even as I melt into his hug, savoring the warmth and solidity of his presence, I'm reminded once again of the special bond we share, the unbreakable tie that binds us together.

Vlad may not be my blood brother, but he's every bit as much an Alexeev as Gavriil or I. Father took him in before I was born, a lost and lonely wolf pup in need of a pack, and he's been a constant presence in my life ever since, a steady rock in the midst of the chaos and turmoil that seems to follow our family wherever we go.

"Gods, I've missed you..." I mumble, my voice muffled against his chest as tears prickle at the corners of my eyes. It's a simple statement, but it carries the weight of all the things I can't say, all the emotions I've been bottling up inside for far too long.

I know Gavriil has always feared that I loved Vlad more. But the truth is, they both hold equal pieces of my heart. Gavriil is my blood, my flesh and bone, the brother I was born to. But Vlad... Vlad is my chosen family, the brother I claimed for myself, and that bond is just as strong, just as unshakable.

As we slowly part, concern flickers in Vlad's expression, his brow furrowing as he takes in the shadows under my eyes, the tight set of my jaw. "Hey..." he purrs, his voice soft and coaxing. "Is everything alright?"

I want to say no. I want to tell him everything, to pour out all the fears and frustrations that have been eating away at me for months now. I want to tell him that our household has become a living hell ever since we left our home in Saint Petersburg, that Gavriil's heart has turned to stone in the wake of Luciana's death, that I feel like I'm suffocating under the weight of his grief and rage.

But I can't. I can't bring myself to burden Vlad with the truth, to shatter the fragile peace of this moment with the harsh realities of my life. So instead, I force a smile onto my face, pushing down the lump in my throat as I pull back to look up at him, my eyes wide with feigned surprise and delight.

"I didn't expect you would come!" I exclaim, the words tumbling out of my mouth in a rush, a desperate attempt to change the subject, to steer the conversation away from the dangerous waters of my own emotions.

Vlad smirks, his silvery eyes twinkling with mischief. "Me neither," he admits, his tone conspiratorial. "The woman practically put me on the plane... D'you think she might have been *that* desperate for some breathing space?"

I can't help but chuckle at that, knowing all too well how overprotective Vlad can be when it comes to his family. "Well, you *can be* a tad overbearing at times..." I tease, but quickly pivot the conversation before I can get myself into trouble. "And my niece? How's the little darling?"

Vlad's face lights up at the mention of his daughter, pride and love radiating from every pore. "She keeps growing!" he gushes, his voice filled with delighted amazement. "My sweet Katya has already spoken her first word—*papa*. She won't say mama yet, and it's been driving Anya mad!"

He laughs, a low, rumbling sound that warms me from the inside out, as he pulls out his cellphone. Instantly, a video appears on the screen, featuring my beautiful baby niece. She's a porcelain doll come to life, with light brown hair and rosy, flushing cheeks. My heart swells with love and longing as I watch her giggle and coo, her tiny hands reaching out towards the camera.

But Vlad tucks the phone away after a moment, his

expression shifting to one of wonder as he takes in our surroundings. "Oh, but enough about me..." he says, his eyes sweeping over the glittering lights and elegant decor of the Deveraux's lawn. "Look at where we're standing. Can you believe it?"

I step back, putting a little distance between us, just enough to meet his stormy gaze. Vlad keeps his arm around my shoulders, a comforting weight that grounds me in the moment. "You seem more than happy about it," I note, a subtle frown creasing my brow.

"I am," Vlad confirms, his voice brimming with satisfaction as he surveys the luminous expanse before us. "This is a great night for our clan—Father would be so proud. Gavriil asked for Cassie's hand in marriage. He's branding her as we speak."

He glances at me sidelong, a hint of mischief curling the corner of his lips, and I feel a flicker of unease in my gut. Something about his words, his tone, doesn't sit right with me.

"Oh?" I murmur, my frown deepening. "Really?"

Vlad leans closer, concern etching itself into the lines of his face. "Does the news displease you, Sam?" he asks, his voice gentle but probing. "Are you not happy for Gavriil?"

I hesitate, the sudden awareness of the game we play in my family hitting me like a ton of bricks. Vlad may be my brother, my confidant, but in this moment, with the weight of politics and power plays hanging heavy in the air, I know I have to choose my words carefully.

"I mean... I am..." I manage, my tongue feeling thick and clumsy in my mouth. "If he loves her."

But even as I say the words, I know they're a lie. Gavriil doesn't love Cassandra, could never love her the way he loved Luciana. His heart, his very soul, belongs to his true mate, now and forever.

Vlad sighs, a flicker of compassion glinting in his eyes. "Love isn't everything, my sweet," he murmurs, his tone gentle but firm.

I feel a surge of irritation at his words, a frustration that he could be so blind to the truth. "But it *is* everything," I insist, my voice rising with each word. "It is. Vlad, I've never seen Gavriil happier than when he was with Luciana."

My brother starts, clearly taken aback by my vehemence. He holds up a cautious hand, his expression troubled. "Sam," he whispers, his voice tinged with melancholy. "Luciana is dead."

The words hit me like a physical blow, stealing the breath from my lungs. I know it's the truth, know that Luciana is gone and never coming back. But the idea that Gavriil should just *move on*, that he should give up on love altogether... it feels wrong, like a betrayal of everything they shared.

"And just because she's dead, is he supposed to give up on love?" I demand, my voice shaking with emotion.

"No, Vlad. That is not right!"

Vlad's eyes widen, worry creasing his brow. In a flash, he's gripping my elbow, steering me away from the crowd, his movements urgent and purposeful. "Please," he murmurs, his voice low and confidential. "Don't mention any of this to Gavriil. It will only hurt him and spoil the evening."

I open my mouth to argue, to make my grievances known, but before I can utter a word, a familiar figure catches my eye. Clarissa Draken, Nik's sister, brushes past us, her presence sending a jolt of electricity through my veins.

If she's here... could Nik be nearby?

My heart leaps into my throat, pounding out a frantic rhythm as my eyes scan the crowd, desperate for any sign of him. I follow Clarissa's movements, tracking her until she disappears into a group of witches, but there's no trace of Nik among them.

Oh, gods. Where is he?

"Are you looking for someone?" Vlad asks, his tone curious, almost knowing.

"No," I breathe, the lie bitter on my tongue. As much as I love my brother, I can't trust him with this. I can't risk him reporting back to Gavriil about my forbidden feelings for Nik.

Suddenly, someone crashes into my shoulder, sending me stumbling forward. "Ow!" I yelp, startled and angry as I whirl around to confront the person responsible.

A woman darts past us, reckless and unabashed, her skin gleaming with the sharpest magic. It's a sight that would go unnoticed by most, but as a witch, I can see the beaming web of power that tangles around her.

My eyes narrow, recognition dawning as I take in the intricate pattern of the magic. "I think that's Gavriil's brand..." I mumble, more to myself than to Vlad.

"What's that?" he asks, leaning in closer to hear me over the din of the party.

"Was that Cassandra Deveraux, Gavriil's chosen mate?" I ask, caution tempering my tone.

Vlad nods, his expression grim. "Yeah, it was."

I scowl, crossing my arms over my chest as I watch Cassandra disappear into the manor. "Well, *she's* in a hurry," I mutter, irritation prickling under my skin. Who does this woman think she is, barging through the crowd like that?

My train of thought is interrupted by a commotion on the other side of the lawn. "Get out of the way!" a familiar voice barks, cutting through the chatter of the guests.

I turn to see Bram Draken shoving his way through the throng of people, his face twisted with anger.

"He looks angry as hell," my brother notes, an eyebrow arching in surprise.

"Mm. Such a *lovely* party," I murmur wryly. And

then, a thought hits me like a bolt of lightning. If Bram is here... then surely, Nik must be with him.

My throat goes dry, my pulse hammering in my ears as I scan the crowd, desperate for a glimpse of those ocean eyes, that tousled blonde hair. But even as I search, a sinking feeling takes root in my gut.

Nik isn't here. I would know if he was, would feel his presence like a physical thing, a tug on my very soul.

As Bram draws closer, I notice something strange about his hands. They're clenched into fists at his sides, glinting with a spectral red light that I've never seen before. Draken magic, pulsing and alive, so different from the golden glow that surrounded Nik that fateful night.

Stark dread claws at my throat as Bram charges towards us, his men following close behind. "Vlad..." I whisper, my voice trembling as I press closer to my brother's side.

Vlad's eyes narrow, a low growl rumbling in his chest as he takes in the approaching threat. In one smooth motion, he steps in front of me, shielding me with his body as he faces down the Draken heir.

I peer around his broad shoulders, my eyes scanning the faces of Bram's entourage, searching for any sign of Nik. But he's not there, and the realization hits me like a punch to the gut.

Face it, Samara. He's not coming. He doesn't care enough to see me, to fight for what we had.

It's over. It's really, truly over.

"Fucking Drakens," Vlad mutters as Bram and his men push past us, disappearing into the manor.

He turns to me, his eyes soft with concern as he takes in my stricken expression. "Are you all right, Sammy?" he asks, his hands coming up to grip my shoulders as he crouches down to my level.

Sometimes, I swear, Vlad still sees me as the little girl I used to be, the baby sister in need of his protection. It's sweet, in a way, but right now, it only serves to make me feel small and fragile, like I might shatter at the slightest touch.

I nod, not trusting myself to speak past the lump in my throat.

"Is there a problem here?" a deep, resonant voice cuts through the air, chilling me to the bone.

"Gavriil!" Vlad exclaims, straightening up and turning to face our brother with a broad grin. "Congratulations, brother."

The Ursa King accepts Vlad's hug with a stiff nod, his expression as burdened and brooding as ever. "Thanks," he mumbles, his voice flat and lifeless. "I'm glad you could make it. I'm leaving."

"You're leaving? But the party has only just begun," Vlad protests, clearly taken aback by Gavriil's abrupt declaration.

But I know better. I've seen the toll that Luciana's

death has taken on my brother, the way he's withdrawn into himself, becoming a mere shadow of the man he used to be. Vlad may not understand, but I do. All too well.

"Samara," Gavriil says, his voice heavy with exhaustion as he turns to me. "You may stay a little longer. Dima will take you home when you're ready."

"I'll take her home," Vlad interjects, squeezing Gavriil's shoulder in a gesture of support. "You go with Dima."

A rush of gratitude washes over me at Vlad's words, at the understanding and compassion that shines in his eyes. He knows, even without being told, that Gavriil needs a moment of solitude, a chance to confront the demons that haunt him in the wake of this ceremony. But Vlad also understands that our brother cannot be left alone, not now, not when the burden of his grief and guilt threatens to crush him.

My heart aches for my brother, for the pain that he carries with him always, the weight of a love lost and a future stolen. "Where are you going?" I ask, my voice small and hesitant.

But Gavriil doesn't answer. He simply turns and walks away, Dima falling into step beside him as they disappear into the manor.

"Vlad, I worry for him..." I mumble, my eyes fixed on the spot where they vanished from view.

"Don't." Vlad pulls me into his arms, his embrace

warm and comforting. "He'll be all right, Sam. Everything's going to be all right now."

But even as he speaks the words, I know they're a lie. Nothing about this feels right, feels like the happy ending we're all pretending it is.

"Because he's marrying a Deveraux witch," I murmur, my gaze vacant and unfocused as I stare out over the glittering lawn.

Is that what awaits me, too? A loveless marriage of convenience, a life spent playing the dutiful wife to a man I barely know? The thought makes my stomach turn, bile rising in my throat.

"Come," Vlad says, offering me his arm with a gentle smile. "I haven't seen you in so long... Let's walk a little."

I manage a faint smile in return, curling my hand around his elbow and allowing him to lead me away from the crowds, into the quiet solitude of the gardens.

But even as we walk, even as I let the beauty of the night wash over me, I can't shake the feeling of emptiness that yawns inside me, the ache of a love lost and a future forever out of reach.

Because Nik is gone, and with him, all my dreams of a happily ever after.

And no matter how hard I try to pretend, no matter how many fake smiles I plaster on my face... I know that nothing will ever be the same again.

28

NIK

I stumble back from my midnight sprint, laden with the burden of sorrow and desire, fear and regret. The suffocating weight threatens to consume me as I struggle to keep moving forward. These past few weeks without Sam have been pure, unadulterated hell. I've lost count of the times I've dialed her number, my finger hovering over the call button, only to hang up before it even rings. I've even contemplated sneaking into the Ursa King's lair, consequences be damned, just to catch a glimpse of her face.

Oh, gods. This is torture.

I've tried to channel my pain into late-night jogs and early morning gym sessions, pushing my body to the brink of exhaustion in a desperate attempt to dull the ache in my soul. But nothing helps. Nothing eases the gaping hole in my chest where Sam used to be.

And tonight, when I had the chance to see her again at the Deveraux's Yule soiree, I forced myself to stay away. It took every ounce of willpower I possessed, every shred of self-control, but I knew that if I laid eyes on my goddess, any restraint I've managed to build up would shatter like glass.

It's for the best, I tell myself, even as my heart screams in protest. Whenever doubt creeps in, whenever I find myself wavering, I just think back to what happened in Brittany, to the terror and pain I saw in Sam's eyes. I never want to hurt her again.

I lean against the kitchen counter, the cool marble pressing into my skin as I catch my breath. The house is quiet, still, a far cry from the chaos that usually reigns within these walls. It's a welcome respite, a moment of peace amidst the storm of my own emotions.

But the silence is short-lived. The rumble of engines shatters the tranquility, the sound growing louder, closer, until it's a roar that echoes through the halls. I push off from the counter, my brow furrowing as I make my way to the window, the water bottle dangling forgotten from my fingertips.

Outside, a convoy of black SUVs tears up the driveway, gravel spraying in their wake. They screech to a halt, the doors flying open before the vehicles have fully stopped. And then Bram is there, erupting from the lead car like a man possessed.

My heart pounds in my chest as I watch him, my

mind racing with the implications of his arrival. I know I should tell him the truth, should confess to the secret that's been eating away at me for days now. But the words stick in my throat, trapped behind the wall of fear and doubt that rises up to choke me. How can I possibly explain what I've become, the beast that lurks beneath my skin, waiting to be unleashed? Will he understand, or will he see me as a monster, a threat to be eliminated?

He moves with a fury that's tangible, his face twisted into a snarl, his eyes wild and blazing. He doesn't speak, doesn't acknowledge the startled looks of the staff as he storms past them, his steps heavy and purposeful as he barrels towards the living room.

I'm moving before I realize it, the water bottle slipping from my grasp and hitting the floor with a dull thud. I don't stop to pick it up. Don't pause to consider the consequences of confronting Bram in this state.

All I know is that something is wrong. Something has happened to put that look on my brother's face. And whatever it is, I need to find out, need to be there to pick up the pieces and try to hold our fractured family together.

So I go after him, my own steps quick and urgent, my heart hammering in my chest as I brace myself for the storm I know is coming. Because if there's one thing I've learned over the years, it's that when Bram is on the warpath, no one is safe. And tonight, I have a feeling that the fallout will be worse than anything we've ever faced before.

"Had a good time at Deveraux Manor?" I ask, raising an eyebrow as I take in his agitated state.

Bram tosses his jacket onto the couch, then makes a beeline for the wine cabinet. "Quite the contrary," he mutters, pouring himself a generous glass of whiskey. "You'll be so glad you didn't come." He knocks back the entire drink in one gulp, his throat working as he swallows.

"Oh?" I move closer, my interest piqued. "How come?"

"That warlock beast, Gavriil... He had the audacity to brand Cassandra." Bram growls, refilling his glass with a shaking hand. "I knew it. I knew he'd sneak into the Deveraux lineage. Gods, I can't stand the fucking bear! Oh, but I'll show him."

A deep frown creases my brow, worry settling like a lead weight in my gut. "Bram, you need to think this through..." I caution, raising a hand in a placating gesture.

But my brother is beyond reason, his temper flaring like a match to kindling. He slams his glass down on the cabinet, his eyes blazing with barely contained rage as they lock onto mine. "I'm going to take my clan to his doorstep and wipe out the entire Alexeev lineage if I have to," he hisses through clenched teeth, "but I will not let this pass!"

Bram strides over to his desk, his movements sharp and jerky, his breath coming in short, harsh pants. He yanks open the top drawer, rummaging through the contents with a ferocity that borders on madness. And then I see it, the glint of metal, the unmistakable shape of a gun.

My blood runs cold, my heart stuttering in my chest as Bram snatches up the weapon, his fingers curling around the grip with a familiarity that terrifies me. "My magic may not be as strong as the *great* Ursa King's…" He checks the chamber, the click of the bullets echoing in the sudden silence. "But I'd *love* to see him dodge one of these." And then he's shoving the gun into his waistband, the bulge of it barely noticeable beneath his tailored shirt.

He turns back to me, his eyes glittering with a dangerous light, a smile that's more of a grimace stretching his lips. "What, now? You gonna try to stop me, little brother?" he taunts, his voice low and mocking. "You gonna stand in my way?"

My jaw clenches, my hands curling into fists at my sides. I know I should back down, should try to diffuse the situation before it escalates any further. But the rage that's been simmering inside me for weeks, the frustration and the pain and the goddamn helplessness, it all boils over in that moment, exploding out of me in a torrent of fury.

"Bram!" I roar, my own anger surging to the surface, hot and molten. "Enough with this foolishness!"

My brother's jaw goes slack, shock and disbelief etched into every line of his face. For a moment, he just stares at me, his eyes wide and unseeing, as if he can't quite believe the words that just came out of my mouth.

But then, with a suddenness that startles me, he's moving, closing the distance between us in two quick strides. His hand shoots out, grabbing the front of my shirt and yanking me forward until our faces are mere inches apart.

"What did you just say to me?" he hisses, his breath hot against my skin, the stench of whiskey heavy in the air.

I swallow hard, my heart pounding in my ears, but I refuse to back down. "You heard me," I manage, my voice steady despite the fury that claws at my insides. "This is insane, Bram. You can't just go off half-cocked, guns blazing, and expect everything to work out. You'll get yourself killed, or worse."

And then, just as quickly as it began, Bram releases his grip on my shirt, shoving me away with an unmistakable air of revulsion.

"Don't you dare talk to me like this... I'm the Draken Heir!" Bram's fist swings high, aiming for my face, but I'm faster. I seize his wrist in an iron grip, pushing him back with a force that sends him flying across the room. He slams into the wall with a sickening thud, his body crumpling to the floor in a heap.

For a moment, we both freeze, stunned by the turn of events. But as I stand there, my chest heaving with exertion and barely contained rage, I realize that I've reached my breaking point. I'm done tolerating Bram's childish tantrums, and I refuse to sit back and watch as he sullies our family's reputation.

Each breath sears my lungs, my heart pounding a furious rhythm against my ribs. Waves of heat wash over me, prickling my skin and blurring my vision.

Bram scrambles to his feet, his expression morphing from shock and anger to pure, unadulterated dread. I don't know what he sees when he looks at me, but I can hazard a guess.

He stumbles back, retreating through the sliding doors and onto the terrace. I follow, my steps measured and deliberate, my anger simmering just beneath the surface.

"Ever since you became the head of this family, I've seen you do nothing but put our bloodline to shame," I begin, my voice low and deadly. Bram backs away, his feet carrying him down the steps and onto the vast expanse of the lawn. "You drink and go to lavish parties. You spend our inheritance as if it were everlasting. I have watched you waste and plunder our family's assets, while successfully dragging our household name through the mud..."

I blink, trying to clear the haze from my vision, but it only grows thicker, more opaque. Still, I push forward, joining my brother in the courtyard, my anger propelling me onward.

"You almost got yourself killed by the Ursa King on a foolish whim!" I snarl, my breaths coming hard and fast. "I've had enough of this, Bram. You're stepping down. Do you hear me?"

Bram's face drains of color, but he manages to force out a defiant reply. "I will do no—such—thing."

Slowly, deliberately, I tilt my head to the side, my eyes narrowing to slits. "I don't think you understand. I'm not giving you a choice here."

Another wave of heat crashes over me, searing my veins and setting my nerves alight. Bram's eyes widen in horror, his mouth falling open in a silent scream. "W— What's happening to you?" he stammers, his voice thin and reedy with fear.

I glance down at my hands, my breath catching in my throat as I see the skin glowing red, the light pulsing from within like a living thing. Before my eyes, my fingernails elongate into razor-sharp talons, my flesh hardening and layering with glimmering golden scales.

I'm shifting. Again. So fucking soon. Sam said it wouldn't happen for a long while, but this... this is different. This time, I'm fully aware of the change, my mind clear and focused even as my body transforms.

I feel the eyes of the clan upon me, hundreds of faces peering down from the terrace, watching in awe and terror as I shed my human skin and become something... other.

Moonlight spills over me, casting my dragon's shadow across the lawn, engulfing Bram's cowering form. Darkness threatens to swallow me whole, to drag me down into the depths of my beast's consciousness, but I fight it, clinging to my sense of self with every ounce of strength I possess.

My dragon is restless, eager to assert its dominance, to unleash its fury upon the world. And for once, I let it, taking a backseat as the beast surges to the forefront of my mind.

A rumbling growl builds in my throat, a roar that shakes the very foundations of the earth. It's a declaration of strength, of power, a warning to all who would dare to challenge me.

I slam my foot down, and the ground trembles beneath me, cracks spiderwebbing out from the point of impact.

That's enough, I tell the beast, struggling to regain control, to pull myself back from the brink. *Go to sleep now.*

But the dragon fights me, screeching its defiance, its hunger for destruction. Fire builds in my throat, searing hot and deadly, and for a terrifying moment, I'm sure I'm going to lose control, going to incinerate everything and everyone in my path.

No, no...! I growl, wrestling with the beast inside me. *Don't do it!* I wrench my head back, and flames erupt from my jaws, shooting upwards into the night sky in a blistering column of heat and light.

Screams of horror rise from the grounds, the clan scattering like frightened rabbits before a predator.

I said... I roar, my voice thundering through my mind. *Go to sleep!*

At last, the dragon relents, its presence diminishing as I assert my will, my dominance. The fire in my veins recedes, the scales fading back into smooth, human skin.

Cold washes over me, and I feel lighter, as if a great weight has been lifted from my shoulders. My knees buckle, and I sink to the ground, my breaths coming in ragged gasps.

When I open my eyes, I'm myself again, my shadow no more than that of a man. A long, shuddering sigh escapes my lips, exhaustion seeping into my bones. But even through the fatigue, I feel a flicker of triumph, of pride.

I did it. I controlled the shift, bent the beast to my will. Sam was right—it *does* get easier with time.

Slowly, painfully, I drag myself to my feet, my eyes seeking out Bram's face in the crowd. He stands frozen at the base of the stairs, his expression a mask of unmitigated horror.

Silence hangs heavy in the air, thick and oppressive. I'm the one to break it, my voice ringing out clear and strong. "You will step down as head of the Draken clan, brother. I'm taking care of the family affairs from now on."

With that, I make my way back to the house, my chest heaving with the effort of each breath. Gods, I need to lie down, to rest, to process the enormity of what just happened.

But Bram's voice stops me in my tracks, cold and bitter as a winter wind. "Do you want to know *why* I got rid of you when you were a child?"

I glance back, confusion furrowing my brow. "You wanted me to go to school, to procure my education..." I manage, the words feeling hollow and inadequate.

"No. It was never that." Bram slips his hands into his pockets, his expression hardening into a mask of cruelty. "I would not share a roof with my parents' killer."

The words hit me like a physical blow, snapping my head back as if he'd struck me. "What are you saying?" I breathe, my voice barely more than a whisper.

Bram steps forward, emboldened by my shock, my pain. "I'm saying exactly that. *You killed our parents.*"

Anger surges through me, white-hot and blinding.

"You're drunk," I snarl, turning away, desperate to escape the venom dripping from his tongue.

"You don't remember, do you?" he taunts, his voice following me up the steps, burrowing into my brain like a parasite. "It didn't come to you? Not even when you were in the beach house?" A pause, heavy with malice. "Oh, you loved playing with fire, Niky. Always experimenting, wielding the flames... That night, you started one. It got out of control and took our parents' lives."

My throat constricts, my vision blurring with unshed tears. "No..." I choke out, the word barely more than a broken whisper.

"The fire came from *you*," Bram continues, relentless, merciless. "Embers set off from your hands and brought us nothing but tragedy and ruin." He shakes his head, a mocking smile twisting his lips. "I knew then you'd be nothing but trouble. And I was right... You're a fucking monster."

Tears spill down my cheeks, hot and scalding. "You're lying," I manage, my voice breaking on the last word.

"Am I, Niky?" Bram raises an eyebrow, his expression one of cruel indolence. "Well... I guess you'll never know."

With that, he brushes past me, striding into the house with the self-satisfied air of a man who knows he's won.

I stand there, frozen, my mind reeling with the

implications of his words. It can't be true. It's impossible. I would never... I could never...

But even as I try to deny it, even as I cling to the fragile hope that Bram is lying, a terrible certainty settles in the pit of my stomach.

I killed my parents.

The knowledge crashes over me like a tidal wave, dragging me under, drowning me in a sea of grief and guilt and self-loathing.

A roar of anguish tears from my throat, raw and primal, a sound of pure, unbridled agony. And as I sink to my knees on the cold, hard ground, I feel something inside me shatter, something vital and irreplaceable.

Because if Bram is telling the truth, if I'm really the one responsible for the death of the two people I loved most in this world... Then maybe I am a monster, after all.

And maybe I deserve to be alone, to live with the weight of my sins for the rest of my miserable life.

Maybe losing Sam, losing everything that ever mattered to me...

Maybe it's no more than I deserve.

29

NIK

A week has passed since I last shifted into my dragon, since the night that changed everything. Bram left that very evening, taking a handful of loyal clan members and his Enforcer with him. But the majority chose to stay, to pledge their loyalty to me as the new head of the Draken family. The time has come to forge my own legacy worthy of pride.

I sit at the desk, my eyes scanning the long list of expenses and investments that Bram made in the last month alone. The numbers are staggering, the sheer amount of money he's blown through enough to make my head spin. I smooth a hand over my mouth, a deep sense of dissatisfaction settling in the pit of my stomach. How could he have been so reckless, so irresponsible with our family's legacy?

One of my first acts as leader was to fire Bram's

accountants, to rid our clan of the incompetent fools who not only failed at their jobs but actively stole from us, lining their own pockets while our coffers dwindled. The betrayal stings, but not as much as the knowledge that I let it happen, that I stood by and did nothing while my brother ran our family name into the ground.

I close the ledger with a snap, the weight of my new responsibilities settling heavily on my shoulders. Tomorrow, I'll meet with a new team of actuaries, professionals who will treat our finances with the respect and diligence they deserve. From now on, I'll be supervising only, delegating the day-to-day tasks to those better suited to handle them. The gods know I have enough on my plate as it is, enough commitments to keep and grudges to fix, all thanks to Bram's quick temper and poor judgment.

Word of my transformation has spread like wildfire through the magical world, whispers of the Last Dragon Shifter, the Draken Firebreather, reaching the ears of every major family. In a matter of days, I've become a legend, a figure of awe and fear and respect. It's a heady feeling, knowing that I've done right by my lineage, that I've owned up to who and what I am.

But even as I bask in the glow of my newfound power, even as I relish the way the tables have turned in my family's favor... I can't shake the weight of my own sins, the burden of the secrets that Bram laid at my feet.

His last words to me, the accusation that I killed our

parents... It haunts me, echoing in my mind like a twisted lullaby. I try to recall that night, to dredge up some memory of what happened, but all I find are brief flashes, hazy images that slip through my grasp like smoke.

Did Bram speak the truth? Was the lethal firemagic that took my parents' lives born from my hands? Or perhaps my dragon, the beast that's lain dormant inside me for so long, somehow broke free that fateful evening, unleashing the blaze that destroyed everything I held dear? Is that why I can't remember, why the events of that night are nothing more than a blank void in my mind?

A low growl rumbles in my chest, frustration and self-loathing warring within me. I shake my head, trying to banish the grim thoughts, but they cling to me like a second skin, tormenting me with possibilities too horrific to contemplate. This is exactly what Bram wanted, I realize with a sinking feeling. He may have lost the reins of our family, but his final blow was a masterful one, a poison that seeps into my very soul, corroding me from the inside out.

The chime of my phone snaps me out of my dark musings, and I glance down at the screen, seeing the reminder for tomorrow's meeting with the new accountants. I heave a sigh, swiping away the notification... and that's when I see it.

The photo memory section, a collage of images

from my weekend with Sam. My breath catches in my throat as I flip through them, each one a bittersweet reminder of the happiness we shared. There we are, walking hand in hand on the beach in Brittany, the sun setting behind us in a blaze of orange and gold. And there, blowing out the candles on my birthday cake, Sam's face lit up with laughter and love.

I linger on a selfie of us kissing, my heart clenching with a longing so intense it steals the air from my lungs. Gods, I miss her. Miss the warmth of her smile, the fire in her eyes, the way she fit so perfectly in my arms. My fierce Little Bear, the woman who taught me what it means to love with every fiber of your being.

I was a fool to let her go, to push her away in some misguided attempt to protect her from the chaos of my life. I see that now, with a clarity that borders on painful. I should have fought for her, should have done everything in my power to be the man she deserved, the partner she needed by her side.

But is it too late? Have I lost my chance at happiness, at the future we might have together?

A knock on the door shatters my thoughts, and I look up, startled. "Come in," I call out, my voice rough with emotion.

The door swings open, and there, standing on the threshold, is my sister. Clarissa. I sent for her, summoning her from London where Bram had settled her, far from the heart of our family.

I rise from my seat, my heart pounding as I take in the sight of her. She's grown so much in the years since I last saw her, no longer the little girl I remember, but a young woman, beautiful and strong. But there's a wariness in her eyes, a guarded look that speaks of the pain and loneliness she's endured.

"Clarissa," I murmur, my voice thick with emotion. "Thank you for coming."

She nods, stepping into the room with a hesitance that breaks my heart. "Nikolaas," she says, my name sounding strange and unfamiliar on her tongue. "You wanted to see me?"

"I did." I take a deep breath, trying to find the right words, the ones that will bridge the gulf between us. "I know we don't really know each other, that we've been apart for so long. But you're my sister, Clarissa. My blood. And I want you to come home, to be a part of this family again."

Her eyes widen, surprise and hope warring on her face. "You mean it?" she whispers, her voice trembling. "You want me to stay?"

"More than anything," I tell her, pouring every ounce of sincerity into my words. "I know it won't be easy, that we have a lot of lost time to make up for. But I'm willing to try if you are."

Tears well in her eyes, spilling over onto her cheeks, and then she's launching herself into my arms, her small frame shaking with sobs. I hold her close, stroking her hair and murmuring words of comfort, my own eyes burning with unshed tears.

"I've never had a real home," she chokes out, her face buried in my chest. "Not since Mum and Dad died. I was always sent away, passed around like an unwanted burden."

"Never again," I vow, my arms tightening around her. "You belong here, Clarissa. With me, with our family. And I swear, I'll do everything in my power to make sure you never feel alone or unwanted again."

We stay like that for a long moment, clinging to each other like lifelines in a storm-tossed sea. And when we finally pull apart, I feel lighter somehow, as if a weight has been lifted from my shoulders.

But then Clarissa's eyes meet mine, and I see something there that makes my blood run cold. A knowing, a sadness that seems to reach into the very depths of my soul.

"You're in terrible pain," she murmurs, her voice soft but filled with a quiet strength. "I can feel it, rolling off you in waves."

I start, my eyes widening in surprise. "How did you...?"

"I'm a witch," she explains, a hint of pride coloring her words. "And an empath, like Mum was. But I'm also a seer, Nik. I see things, things that haven't happened yet, but will."

I swallow hard, my heart racing in my chest. "And

what do you see now?" I ask, my voice barely above a whisper.

Clarissa's gaze turns distant, unfocused, as if she's looking at something far away. "I see her," she breathes, her voice taking on a dream-like quality. "Samara Alexeeva. *Your fated mate.* You're destined for each other, Nik. Two halves of the same soul, bound together by a love that transcends time and space."

I stumble back, my knees suddenly weak, my mind reeling with the implications of her words. Sam... my fated mate? The idea seems impossible, too good to be true. And yet, as I think back on our time together, on the way she made me feel, the way everything just seemed to click into place when I was with her...

It makes sense. Perfect, beautiful sense.

Of course she's my destined mate. How could I have ever doubted it, ever questioned the bond between us? Everything always felt so natural, so right when we were together, as if the universe itself had conspired to bring us into each other's lives.

"Will you fight for her, Nik?" Clarissa asks, her eyes boring into mine, searching my face for an answer. "Will you do whatever it takes to win her back, to claim the future that's meant to be yours?"

And in that moment, I know. Know with a certainty that goes bone-deep, that reaches into the very core of my being.

"Yes," I breathe, my voice ringing with conviction,

with a determination that sets my soul on fire. "Yes, I will fight for her. For us. For the love that we share, the love that nothing and no one can destroy."

Clarissa smiles, a fierce, proud smile that makes my heart swell with affection. "Good," she says, reaching out to take my hand in hers. "Because you're going to need every ounce of that strength, every bit of that courage, if you're going to face what's coming."

I frown, a flicker of unease running through me at her words. "What do you mean? What's coming?"

But she just shakes her head, her expression turning serious, almost grim. "Darkness," she whispers, her voice taking on a haunting, otherworldly quality. "A storm that threatens to consume everything in its path, to destroy all that we hold dear."

I feel a chill run down my spine, a sense of foreboding that settles heavy in my gut. But I push it aside, squaring my shoulders and lifting my chin in defiance.

"Let it come," I growl, my eyes flashing with the fire of my dragon, the power that thrums through my veins. "Whatever it is, whatever challenges lie ahead... I'll face them head-on. I'll fight with every breath in my body, every beat of my heart, to protect the ones I love."

Clarissa nods, a fierce light shining in her eyes. "And we'll be right there beside you," she vows, her hand tightening around mine. "Your family, your clan. We'll stand with you, Nik. Always."

A torrent of gratitude overwhelms me, a love so

fierce that it takes my very breath away. This is everything I've ever yearned for. A clan to call my own, a cause to fight for, a purpose to live and die for.

And Sam... my beautiful, beloved Sam. My fated mate, the other half of my soul.

I'll prove to her that our love is stronger than any obstacle, any force that dares to stand in our way.

Come what may, I'll find my way back to her.

It's late in the evening. New Year's Eve. It's just me and my brothers, stuck in the house, watching each other's dull faces. Otherwise, the manor is empty. Gavriil sent everyone away. We might be miserable, but our clan deserves a bit of cheer in their lives.

I wander into the parlor, my mind still reeling from the events of the night, from the strange mix of emotions that swirl inside me like a brewing storm. And that's when I see him, sprawled out on the couch like he doesn't have a care in the world.

Vlad is laughing, his face lit up with a joy that I haven't seen in ages. He's got his phone propped up on his chest, and I can hear the tinny sound of voices coming through the speaker. As I move closer, I catch a glimpse of the screen, my heart melting at the sight that greets me.

It's Anya, her face radiant with happiness as she cradles their baby girl in her arms. Katya is babbling away, her chubby little hands reaching out towards the camera, towards her daddy. And Vlad... gods, the look on his face as he coos and makes silly faces at his daughter. It's enough to bring tears to my eyes.

For a moment, I just stand there, watching them, drinking in the pure, unadulterated love that flows between them. It's a beautiful thing, a reminder of the good that still exists in this world, even amidst all the darkness and chaos.

But then Katya starts to fuss, her little face scrunching up as she lets out a wail that pierces the air. Anya murmurs something soothing, bouncing the baby gently in her arms as she turns back to the camera.

"I think someone's ready for her nap," she says, her voice soft and apologetic. "We should probably let you go, babe."

Vlad's face falls, but he nods in understanding. "Give her a kiss for me, will you?" he asks, his tone wistful. "And tell her *papa* loves her, more than anything in this world."

"I will," Anya promises, blowing him a kiss of her own before ending the call.

Vlad sighs, staring down at the blank screen for a long moment before he seems to realize I'm there. He sits up, running a hand through his hair as he shoots me a sheepish grin.

"Sorry about that," he says, tossing his phone aside. "I just... I miss them, you know? Miss seeing my little girl grow up, miss being there for all the little moments."

I nod, my heart aching for him, for the sacrifice he's making to be here, to support our family in this time of need. "I know," I murmur, moving to sit beside him on the couch. "But you're doing the right thing, Vlad. You're being a good brother, a good son. And Anya and Katya, they understand that. They love you all the more for it."

He gives me a grateful smile, bumping his shoulder against mine in a gesture of affection. "Thanks, Sam. I don't know what I'd do without you, you know that? You're the glue that holds this crazy family together."

I snort, shaking my head. "I don't know about that. Feels more like I'm the one who's falling apart these days."

Vlad frowns, his brow creasing with concern. "Hey," he says softly, taking my hand in his. "You want to talk about it? I know things have been rough lately, with everything that's going on. But you know I'm here for you, right? Always."

Of course, I know. Secretly, I think I'm the reason he's stuck around here for so long—me, not Gavriil.

I squeeze his hand, blinking back the sudden sting

of tears. "I know," I whisper, my voice thick with emotion. "And I appreciate that, more than you know. But right now... I think I just need a distraction. Something to take my mind off all the craziness, even if it's just for a little while."

Vlad nods, a glimmer of understanding in his eyes. "Should we do something?" he asks, his tone light and casual, but I can hear the underlying warmth, the unspoken offer of companionship.

I open my mouth to respond, to tell Vlad that yes, I'd love to do something, anything, to escape the suffocating weight of my own thoughts. But before I can utter a word, the sound of footsteps echoes from the hallway, heavy and measured, a cadence I'd know anywhere.

Gavriil.

I sit up straighter, my heart racing as I watch my brother enter the parlor, his face a mask of carefully controlled calm. But I can see the tension in his shoulders, the tightness around his eyes, the way his jaw clenches as he takes in the sight of Vlad and me, huddled together on the couch like conspirators.

For a moment, he just stands there, his gaze flickering between us, and I feel a pang of unease, wondering if he's going to say something, if he's going to demand to know what we were talking about. But then he simply nods, a curt acknowledgment of our presence, before crossing the room to the bar cart in the corner.

I watch as he pours himself a drink, the amber liquid sloshing against the sides of the glass as he lifts it to his lips. He downs it in one gulp, grimacing slightly at the burn, before setting the glass back down with a decisive clink.

And then he's moving again, striding towards us with a purposeful air that sets my nerves on edge. He sinks down onto the couch beside me, close enough that I can feel the heat of his body, the coiled power that thrums just beneath the surface of his skin.

The silence stretches between us, thick and heavy, and I find myself holding my breath, waiting for the inevitable explosion, the outpouring of anger and grief and bitter recrimination that I know is coming.

But it never does.

Instead, Gavriil just sits there, his eyes fixed on some distant point, his expression inscrutable. And slowly, gradually, I feel the tension begin to drain from the room, replaced by a strange sense of calm, of shared understanding.

At least as we sit here in the parlor, we bear no masks. There's no pretense. No politics. It reminds me of the times we had when the three of us lived under the same roof in Saint Petersburg, before the world went to hell and took our happiness with it.

Back then, we were just siblings, bound by love and

loyalty and the unshakable knowledge that we would always have each other's backs, no matter what. And for a moment, as I sit there sandwiched between my brothers, I can almost believe that nothing has changed, that we're still those same people, still capable of weathering any storm as long as we're together.

Oh, how I long to go home, to return to the familiar comfort of Saint Petersburg and the life we had before everything fell apart. But now that Gavriil has branded Cassandra, we're stuck in Paris for the foreseeable future, trapped in a gilded cage of duty and obligation.

There was a time when I would have given anything to live here, to immerse myself in the glittering world of art and fashion and endless possibility. But now... now it all feels hollow, a shiny veneer hiding the rot and decay beneath.

I release a long, weary sigh, sinking deeper into the plush leather sofa as I run my fingers back and forth over my gown, the repetitive motion soothing in its mindlessness.

"Any plans for tonight, brother?" Vlad asks, breaking the heavy silence that hangs over the room.

"None," Gavriil replies, his tone curt and dismissive. Lazily, he picks up a WIRED magazine from the coffee table, his glazed eyes barely registering the words on the page. I know he's not really reading, just going through the motions, his mind no doubt whirring with plans and schemes, always three steps ahead of the rest of us.

"What about you, Sam?" Vlad turns to me, his eyebrows arching softly, his expression gentle and inviting. He's always been like this with me, all heart and warmth, the wolf to Gavriil's bear.

"No plans tonight," I mutter, the words tasting sour on my tongue. Gods, when did I become so bitter, so jaded? I'm moping and brooding just like Gavriil, a realization that sends a shudder of disgust through me. Have I really sunk so low?

"Then I'm sure we must come up with something," Vlad says, his smile bright and hopeful, a valiant attempt to lighten the oppressive atmosphere. But it's futile, a band-aid on a gaping wound. Everything feels bleak and pointless these days, a never-ending cycle of misery and frustration.

A knock on the door shatters the stillness, and Gavriil grunts in annoyance, rolling his eyes as he folds the magazine and tosses it aside. He slumps back on the sofa, his posture the very picture of royal ennui.

I scowl, turning to Vlad with a silent plea, but he just leans back, his stormy eyes meeting mine with a knowing look. The corner of his mouth twitches, a hint of a smirk that says, "You know I'm not getting that, right?"

Another knock, more insistent this time, and I feel my patience snap like a frayed thread.

I suck at my teeth, rising from my seat with a huff of irritation. "A little chivalry would be nice now and then," I grumble under my breath as I march towards the door, my footsteps heavy with resentment.

It's infuriating, the way they treat me. "Too mighty and kingly to open a door? Ugh!" I mutter, my hand closing around the lock with more force than necessary.

But as I turn the key and pull the door open, all thoughts of annoyance and frustration flee my mind, replaced by a shock so profound it steals the breath from my lungs.

Because there, standing on the other side of the threshold, is Nik.

My Nik.

31

SAM

"Nik," I breathe, my fingers tightening on the door handle, my knees threatening to give out beneath me. His name falls from my lips like a prayer, a plea, a desperate attempt to make sense of the impossible sight before me.

"Sam," he whispers back, ice-blue eyes locking onto mine with an intensity that steals my breath. He licks his lower lip, a nervous gesture that sends a shiver down my spine, and I find myself drinking in every detail of his face, from the chiseled line of his jaw to the perfect slope of his nose. And gods, that scent—that glorious, intoxicating cologne that clings to his skin, making my head spin and my heart race.

His hair is longer now, falling in tousled waves that beg for my fingers to run through them. It suits him, this new look—a little wild, a little untamed, like the man himself.

But then reality comes crashing back in, the shock of his presence hitting me like a punch to the gut. What is he doing here, at my house, with my brothers just a few rooms away?

Panic claws at my throat, my eyes widening as I hiss out a warning. "You can't be here!"

But Nik doesn't flinch, doesn't back down. Instead, he presses his hand against the door, pushing it open with a slow, deliberate motion that brooks no argument.

He's not leaving. And gods help me, I don't want him to.

I cling to the door, my throat going dry as he steps inside, his presence filling the hallway like a physical thing. "Nik?" I whisper, my voice barely more than a breath. "What are you doing?"

He stops in the middle of the hall, turning to face me with a look that steals the air from my lungs. "Where is your brother?" he asks softly, his tone low and intimate, meant for my ears alone.

"M-My brother?" I stammer, my mind reeling. "My *brothers* are in the parlor." Gods, Nik, take a hint! Run, before it's too late!

But he doesn't run. Instead, he nods, his eyebrows lifting slightly, his eyes filled with a longing so pure and undisguised it makes my heart ache. He purses his lips, and that dimple, that sinful little divot in his left cheek, winks at me, tempting me to lean in and press my mouth against it.

Focus, Samara! Nik is here, in your home, with both of your brothers just a few steps away. Is he mad? Does he have a death wish?

But as he takes a step forward, his gaze never leaving mine, I find myself moving with him, my arm lifting of its own accord to point down the hallway. He bows his head in silent acknowledgment, falling into step beside me as we make our way towards the parlor.

I don't know why I'm doing this, why I'm going along with his insanity. My heart is pounding so hard I'm sure he can hear it, the blood rushing in my ears like a roaring tide.

As we reach the doorway, my breath catches in my throat, a wave of dizziness washing over me. I think I might faint, or throw up, or both.

"Sam?" Vlad's voice cuts through the haze, his tone laden with concern as he rises from the couch. "Are you unwell?"

But then his eyes land on Nik, and his expression morphs into one of pure, unadulterated fury. Gavriil must have told him about what happened, about the forbidden bond between Nik and me—but Vlad, sweet, kind Vlad, would never bring it up, not if it meant causing me pain.

The silence stretches, heavy and oppressive, until Gavriil finally looks up, his gaze drawn by the tension in the room. And when he sees Nik standing there, his face flushes with rage, his features hardening into a mask of barely contained violence.

"What are you doing here?" he roars, surging to his feet and crossing the room in three long strides, until he's standing toe-to-toe with Nik, their faces mere inches apart.

But Nik doesn't flinch, doesn't back down. He meets Gavriil's glare head-on, his resolve unwavering in the face of my brother's wrath. "I'd like to speak with you," he says, his voice calm and even, betraying none of the turmoil that must be raging inside him—*if there is any.*

Gavriil starts, his eyes widening in surprise, as if he's just realized something. He growls, a sound of pure frustration, and heaves a sigh that seems to come from the very depths of his soul. "Given recent *events*, I fear I'm forced to hear whatever you have to say," he mutters through clenched teeth.

And then he does something that leaves me speechless, something I never thought I'd see in a million years.

Gavriil, the mighty Ursa King, steps aside, allowing Nik to enter the parlor.

I stand there in the hallway, my mind reeling, my wrist aching from the force of my own grip. What is happening? What could Nik possibly have to say that would make Gavriil listen, that would earn him an audience with the man who hates him more than anyone else in the world?

"Sam," Nik says, his voice cutting through the chaos of my thoughts. "You should come too."

I blink, my mouth opening and closing like a fish out of water. But somehow, I manage to nod, my feet carrying me into the room as if of their own accord.

Gavriil drags the sofa in front of the fireplace, his movements sharp and angry, while Vlad pulls an armchair up beside him. And then there's just the couch left, the only spot big enough for two.

For Nik and me.

We sit, the heat of his body seeping into mine, and I feel like I'm going to combust, like I'm going to shatter into a million pieces from the sheer intensity of the moment.

"Your brother stepped down as head of the family, I hear," Gavriil begins, his voice deceptively calm, a silken threat hidden beneath the veneer of civility.

"He did," Nik confirms, his posture relaxed, his demeanor unruffled. I envy his composure, the way he seems to take everything in stride, even as my nerves are stretched tight as a bowstring.

"A smart choice," Gavriil says, a hint of grudging respect in his tone. "Bram's not cut out for it. Never will be." He pauses, fiddling with his cufflinks in a gesture that's as much a power play as it is a nervous tic. "And will you do a better job at it, I wonder?"

Nik's lips curve in the ghost of a smile, his eyes glinting with a newfound confidence that sends a shiver down my spine. "I'll try," he says simply, and in that moment, I believe him. I believe that he'll move heaven and earth to be the leader his people need, to bring honor and glory back to the Draken name.

Vlad's gaze darts between Nik and me, his brow furrowed in confusion and concern. But he says nothing, deferring to Gavriil's authority as always. In the end, the crown trumps all.

"Have you come here to threaten me?" Gavriil asks bluntly, cutting through the pretense and the posturing to get to the heart of the matter.

"No," Nik replies, his voice quiet but firm. "I came here to settle our grudges once and for all."

My brothers exchange a look of surprise and amusement, their eyebrows climbing towards their hairlines in perfect unison.

"Huh," Vlad says, a smirk playing at the corners of his mouth. "Indeed, you are naïve."

But Nik just leans forward, steepling his fingers in a gesture of calm deliberation. "I will put a stop to any violence from my clan to yours," he declares, his words ringing with the weight of a vow. "And I assure you, any disruptions to my law will be severely punished."

Gavriil shoots him a look of pure incredulity, his eyes narrowing to slits. "You'll *burn* them, perhaps?" he asks, his tone as dry as the Sahara.

"Maybe," Nik concedes, matching my brother's sarcasm with a cool nonchalance that makes my heart swell with pride. "Can I expect the same assurance from you, Ursa King?"

Gavriil raises his chin, studying Nik with a new intensity, a begrudging fascination that borders on respect. And I sit there, my mind whirling, trying to make sense of the sudden shift in the room, the way the tide seems to be turning before my very eyes.

Why am I even here? I wonder, my presence feeling more and more superfluous by the second. This is politics, the dance of power and alliances that I've never been a part of, never had a say in.

"Will you challenge my claim to the Deveraux Witch?" Gavriil asks, his voice carefully neutral, betraying none of the emotion that must be churning beneath the surface.

"I will not," Nik replies, and I feel a rush of relief so strong it makes me dizzy. At least there will be peace between our families, a truce that's been a long time coming.

"Then we have an agreement." Gavriil rises from his seat, his hands smoothing over the arms of the sofa in a gesture of finality. The meeting is over, and with it, the tenuous courtesy he's extended to Nik.

I heave a sigh, pushing myself to my feet, ready to show Nik out and try to salvage what's left of my dignity. But then he speaks again, his words freezing me in place like a deer caught in headlights.

"There's something else," he says, his tone even, almost casual, as if he's not about to drop a bombshell that will change everything.

"Oh?" Gavriil cocks his head, his eyes narrowing in suspicion.

"I would like your permission to date Samara," Nik continues, and my heart stops beating, my breath catching in my throat as the world seems to tilt on its axis.

Did he really just say that? Am I dreaming, or have I finally lost my mind?

But no, it's real, it's happening, and the look on Gavriil's face is one of pure, unadulterated shock.

"You—what?" Vlad sputters, his composure cracking like a pane of glass.

"No," Gavriil snaps, his voice harsh and unyielding.

But Nik doesn't back down, doesn't falter. "I love her," he says simply, his eyes finding mine, holding me captive with the depth of emotion I see there. "And I believe she feels the same way."

Gavriil flinches as if he's been slapped, his gaze darting to me, searching my face for confirmation, for denial, for something. "Samara?" he asks, his voice strained, almost pleading.

And I nod, a tiny, barely perceptible movement that feels like the greatest act of defiance I've ever committed. Because it's true, it's always been true, and I'm done hiding it, done pretending that my heart doesn't beat for Nik and Nik alone.

"Gavriil," Vlad hisses, his tone a warning, a reminder of the line we're crossing, the taboo we're shattering.

But my brother just takes a hand to his brow, his fingers massaging the tension there. "I know, Volodya," he mutters, his voice rough with resignation. "I know." He looks away, his hand sliding down to cover his mouth, a telltale sign that he's holding back, that he's fighting the urge to speak his mind.

And then he's turning back to Nik, his eyes hard and unyielding. "You're a fucking *dragon*," he says, his tone dripping with venom. "Do I even have a say in this?"

Nik tilts his head, a shrug rippling through his broad shoulders. And I know, in that moment, that he's won. That Gavriil, for all his bluster and bravado, is no match for the force of nature that is Nikolaas Draken.

"Yes, you may date," my brother grits out, the words like broken glass in his mouth. "You're bound to split up, anyway. Love never lasts."

But I barely hear him, barely register the bitterness in his voice. Because Nik is rising to his feet, his hand finding mine, his fingers lacing through my own like they were made to fit there.

"Thank you," I breathe, my heart soaring as I cling

to his arm, my fingers digging into the hard muscle beneath his shirt.

Gavriil sneers, waving a dismissive hand in our direction. "Please," he says, his voice dripping with sarcasm. "Spare me the PDA."

Nik frowns, confusion and uncertainty flickering across his face. "The PDA?" he murmurs, glancing down at me for clarification.

I feel my cheeks heat, a blush staining my skin as I bite my lip to keep from grinning like a fool. "Public display of... affection," I explain, my voice barely above a whisper.

"Oh, I see." Nik nods, a slow smile spreading across his face. "I thought I could take her on a date." He turns to me, his ocean eyes boring into mine with an intensity that steals my breath.

"That sounds fun," I blurt out, my heart racing at the thought of spending time with him, of being able to show the world that we're together, that we belong to each other in every way that matters.

"Yeah, yeah," Gavriil mutters, already walking away, his shoulders tense and his jaw clenched. "Do whatever you want."

Vlad follows close behind, but not before shooting me a look that's equal parts warning and concern. I know he's worried about me, about the path I've chosen, but I also know that he'll support me, no matter what. Because that's what family does.

And then it's just Nik and me, alone in the parlor, the air thick with the weight of everything that's just happened. He takes my hands in his, his thumb stroking across my knuckles in a gesture that's so tender, so achingly sweet, that I feel like I might cry.

"I have a surprise for you," he whispers, his voice low and intimate. "Will you come with me?"

"Yes," I breathe, the word tumbling from my lips without a second thought. Because there's nothing in this world that I want more than to be with him, to follow him wherever he leads, to build a life together that's filled with love and laughter and endless possibility.

My fingers tighten around his. A silent promise, a vow that needs no words. And as we walk out of the room, out of the house that's been my prison for so long, I feel a weight lift from my shoulders, a sense of freedom and joy that I've never known before.

Because I'm with Nik. My dragon, my love.

32

NIK

We arrive at my place just before the clock strikes twelve, the anticipation thrumming through my veins like a living thing. I lead Sam to the terrace, my heart pounding with nervous excitement as I watch her, waiting for the moment when she'll discover the surprise I've spent hours preparing.

And then, finally, she sees it—the candle-lined trail of red rose petals, winding like a crimson ribbon through the night, each curve and bend illuminated by the soft, flickering glow of votive candles. The effect is breathtaking, a path of love and light leading towards the surprise that awaits her.

Sam turns to me, her eyes wide with wonder, the candlelight dancing across her face and setting her maroon irises ablaze. A delicate blush stains her cheeks, the color as soft and sweet as the rose petals beneath our feet.

"Nik?" she breathes, her voice soft and full of questions. "What is this?"

I fight back a smile, wanting to savor the look of awe on her face for just a moment longer. "Go on," I tell her, gesturing towards the path, an invitation and a promise all at once.

Together, we move through the garden tunnel, the twinkling amber string-lights casting a warm, romantic glow over everything they touch. And then, at last, we reach the lawn, where the real surprise awaits.

A picnic, laid out on soft wool blankets, complete with a bottle of champagne and the flicker of candlelight. The air is crisp and cool, the night still and full of possibility, and as I watch Sam take it all in, I feel a rush of love so intense it steals my breath.

"Nik..." she whispers, her voice trembling with emotion.

I come up behind her, slipping my hands into my pockets to hide the way they shake. Because this, right here, is everything I've ever wanted, everything I've ever dreamed of. The sheer joy of seeing her happy, of being the one to put that look of wonder on her face... it's a feeling that can't be matched.

Well, almost.

Sam turns to face me, her hand coming up to rest on my chest, and I slide my arm around her waist, pulling her close. The scent of her perfume, roses and vanilla, fills my lungs, and I breathe it in like a drowning man gasping for air.

"You set all this up," she murmurs, her eyes searching mine, a hint of mischief sparkling in their depths. "My brother... he could have said no."

I feel my lips curve into a smile, the tension draining from my body as I recall our earlier triumph. "But he didn't," I point out, gently guiding her to sit on the blanket.

I settle in behind her, wrapping my arms around her and pulling her back against my chest. And gods, the feeling of her in my embrace, the warmth of her body seeping into mine... it's like coming home, like finding a piece of myself I never even knew was missing.

"I will never again let you go," I vow, my lips brushing the shell of her ear. Because it's the truth, the one thing I know with absolute certainty. I've lost her once, and I'll be damned if I ever let it happen again.

Sam melts into my hold, her head falling back onto my shoulder. "I will never again let you," she whispers, and the words are like a balm to my battered soul, a promise that echoes through every fiber of my being.

She shifts in my arms, turning to face me, and suddenly, we're mere inches apart, our breath mingling in the space between us. And in that moment, everything else falls away—the war between our families, the weight of my sins, the chaos of the world beyond this perfect, stolen slice of time.

I'm free. Free to love her, to cherish her, to give her everything I have and everything I am, for as long as she'll let me.

"I have a gift for you," I murmur, reaching into my pocket and pressing the small box into her hand.

Sam glances down, her brow furrowing in confusion as she takes in the familiar red and gold detailing. "Nik..." she starts, her fingers tracing the edges of the case. "Are you returning my birthday present? Didn't you like it?"

I chuckle, shaking my head. "Open it," I urge, my heart racing in my chest as I wait for her reaction.

With a last, uncertain glance in my direction, Sam flips open the lid... and gasps, her eyes widening in shock and wonder.

Because there, nestled in the velvet lining, is a rose gold diamond ring, the metal gleaming softly in the candlelight. The band is adorned with the iconic screw motifs, a symbol of our love's strength and endurance. And there, engraved on the inside, are our names, forever commemorating the unbreakable bond we share.

"Is this...?" she whispers, her voice trailing off as she stares at the ring, her fingers trembling as they hover over the precious metal.

"This is a promise ring," I explain, taking her hand in mine, my thumb stroking over her knuckles in a gesture of reassurance and love. "In my family, in the Draken clan, we seal our promises with diamonds. But these aren't just any ordinary gems, Sam. They're infused with magic, with the very essence of our dragon souls."

I lift the ring from its velvet bed, holding it up so that it catches the light, the diamonds sparkling like captured starlight. "When a Draken gives a diamond to their beloved, it's more than just a symbol of love and commitment. It's a piece of ourselves, a reminder of the unbreakable bond we share."

I slide the ring onto her finger, my heart swelling with emotion as I watch it settle into place, a perfect fit. "This diamond, Sam... it carries a part of me, a fragment of my heart and my magic. It's a promise, not just of my love, but of my protection, my devotion. As long as you wear it, you'll always carry a piece of me with you, no matter where you go or what challenges you face."

Sam's eyes are wide, shimmering with unshed tears as she listens to my words, her fingers curling around mine. "Nik," she breathes, her voice thick with emotion. "I don't know what to say. This is... it's..."

I smile, lifting her hand to my lips and pressing a soft kiss to her knuckles. "You don't have to say anything, love. Just know that I'm yours, body and soul, for as long as you'll have me."

I hesitate for a moment, my heart hammering in my chest as I gather my courage. "Consider it a test flight for when *the next one* comes," I murmur, my voice laden with intimate intensity, promising an experience like no other.

Because as much as I long to drop to one knee, to pledge my life to hers in front of the gods and everyone... I know it's too soon, too much, too fast. I don't want to scare her away, don't want to risk losing her again when I've only just found her.

But this, this small token of my love and devotion... it's a start, a symbol of the future I want to build with her, the life I want to share by her side.

Sam's breath catches, her eyes searching mine for a long, charged moment. And then she's launching herself into my arms, her lips finding mine in a kiss that sets my soul on fire. I respond with equal fervor, pouring every ounce of love and longing into the press of my mouth against hers, the slide of my tongue over the seam of her lips.

When we finally break apart, both of us breathless and flushed, I cup her face in my hands, my eyes boring into hers with an intensity that borders on desperation.

"He's wrong, you know," I murmur, my voice rough with emotion.

Sam blinks, confusion clouding her features. "Who is?"

"Your brother," I clarify, my thumb tracing the delicate arch of her cheekbone. "He's wrong. A dragon's love lasts forever. And I love you, Samara Alexeeva. I love you with my entire being... the man and the dragon."

Tears well in her maroon eyes, spilling over onto her cheeks in glittering tracks. "I love you, Nik," she breathes, leaning into my touch, into the warmth of my embrace.

And then, as if the universe itself is celebrating our love, the clock chimes midnight, heralding the start of a new year. Fireworks explode overhead, painting the sky in a riot of color and light, but I barely notice, too lost in the woman in my arms, in the feel of her lips against mine as I kiss her again, slow and deep and full of promise.

Because this, right here... it's everything. It's a glimpse of the happiness that awaits us, the joy and laughter and endless possibility that stretches out before us like a shining path.

And as I hold Sam close, our hearts beating in perfect sync, I know that I'll never let her go, never stop fighting for the love we've found, the love we've built against all odds.

Come what may, we'll stand side by side. Dragon and bear, fire and ice, two halves of the same soul.

Forever and always.

ABOUT AUTHOR NAME

Silvana G. Sánchez is the USA TODAY bestselling author of sinfully addictive dark fantasy new adult novels *Ash and Snow, Steel and Stone, Written in Blood,* and more paranormal and fantasy romance stories, including the *Vesely Academy* series. She lives in Mexico with her husband, son, and two adorable Shih-Tzu she calls her dragons. When not plotting away in her writing den, she's known to poke eyes in her practice as an ophthalmologist.

For more information:
silvanagsanchez.com
sgs.author@gmail.com

www.ingramcontent.com/pod-product-compliance
Lightning Source LLC
Chambersburg PA
CBHW060656190726

48289CB00002B/440